WILLIAM

SHAKESPEARE'S

—— THE ——
FORCE DOTH AWAKEN

STAR WARS

PART THE SEVENTH

WILLIAM

SHAKESPEARE'S

—— THE ——

FORCE DOTH AWAKEN

STAR WARS°

PART THE SEVENTH

By Ian Doescher

INSPIRED BY THE WORK OF LUCASFILM
AND WILLIAM SHAKESPEARE

QUIRK BOOKS

PHILADELPHIA

Library of Congress Cataloging in Publication Number: 2016961078

ISBN: 978-1-59474-985-8

Printed in the United States of America

Typeset in Sabon

Text by Ian Doescher
Designed by Doogie Horner
Illustrations by Nicolas Delort
Production management by John J. McGurk

Quirk Books
215 Church Street
Philadelphia, PA 19106
quirkbooks.com

10 9 8 7 6 5 4 3 2 1

TO ARACELLI, ADDISON, AND SOPHIE,

THAT YOU MAY GROW TO BE AS STRONG AS REY

DRAMATIS PERSONAE

CHORUS

REY, *a maiden of Jakku*
FN-2187/FINN, *a former stormtrooper*
POE DAMERON, *a pilot of the Resistance*
BB-8, *Poe's droid*
GENERAL LEIA ORGANA, *of the Resistance*
HAN SOLO, *a scoundrel and Leia's husband*
CHEWBACCA, *his Wookiee and first mate*
C-3PO, *a protocol droid*
R2-D2, *his companion*
LUKE SKYWALKER, *a Jedi Knight*
ADMIRAL ACKBAR, ADMIRAL STATURA, MAJOR BRANCE, MAJOR
EMATT, DOCTOR KALONIA, SNAP WEXLEY, NIEN NUNB, YOLO ZIFF,
JESS PAVA, *and* ELLO ASTY, *of the Resistance*
SUPREME LEADER SNOKE, *of the First Order*
KYLO REN, *a dastardly villain of the First Order*
GENERAL HUX, *of the First Order*
CAPTAIN PHASMA, *a trooper of the First Order*
COLONEL KAPLAN, COLONEL DATOO, LIEUTENANT MITAKA, *and*
OFFICERS UNAMO *and* THANNISON, *of the First Order*
LOR SAN TEKKA, *an old man of Jakku*
UNKAR PLUTT, *a trader of Niima Outpost*
TEEDO, *a junker of Jakku*
HAPPABORE, *a beast of Jakku*
BALA-TIK *and* GUAVIAN DEATH GANG, *rogues*
TASU LEECH *and* KANJIKLUB, *scoundrels*
RATHTARS, *jolly monsters*
MAZ KANATA, *a pirate of Takodana*
BAZINE, GRUMMGAR, GA-97, CAPTAIN ITHANO, *and* QUIGGOLD,
patrons of Maz's castle

FIRST ORDER TROOPERS, RESISTANCE PILOTS, DROIDS, RESIDENTS
OF JAKKU, *and* VARIOUS CREATURES

PROLOGUE.

Outer space.

Enter CHORUS.

CHORUS   Luke Skywalker hath sadly disappear'd,
And in his absence come most wicked foes.
The cruel First Order hath made all afeard—
Like phoenix from the Empire's ash it grows.
They shall not rest till Skywalker is dead,   5
Yet others seek to rescue him from harm.
By Leia—General Organa—led,
Th'Republic doth a brave Resistance arm.
Her brother she doth earnestly pursue,
Thus may he help bring peace to restoration.   10
She sends a daring pilot to Jakku,
Where one old friend perchance knows Luke's location.
In time so long ago begins our play,
In yearning galaxy far, far away.

                                        [Exit.

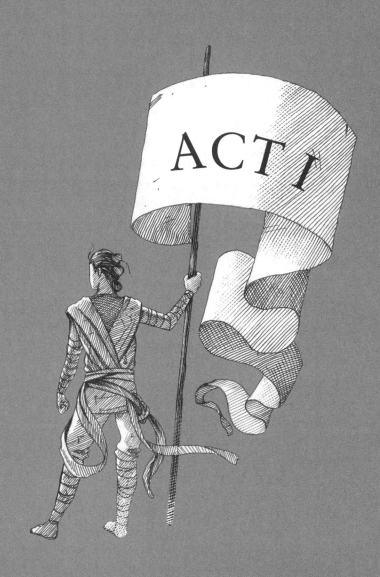

SCENE 1.

On the planet Jakku.

Enter LOR SAN TEKKA.

LOR Alas, you do not meet a man but frowns,
Or so it seems within our galaxy.
For with the rise of this First Order fierce,
The stars cast but a dim and feeble light.
Or thus it is to one as old as I,   5
Who hath seen much within my span of years:
The phantom menace, which did shake each soul,
The vast clone army, which made bold attack,
The Sith's revenge upon the Jedi true,
The small but bold new hope the rebels brought,   10
The way the vicious Empire did strike back,
The grand return the Jedi then did make.
Mine eyes were witness to the fair result:
Decline and fall of the Galactic Empire.
What follow'd, though, did beggar all belief: 15
The swift destruction of the chronicles
Wherewith the New Republic would bring calm,
Suppression of the Jedi history
And ev'ry story of their gallantry,
The rise of the most vile First Order, which,   20
E'en now, doth move upon my home, Jakku.
Their mighty ships I spy beyond the skies,
Like doomsday keenly waiting in the wings.
Our galaxy doth exorcism need
From this pernicious blight upon its face.   25

My hope is that the brave Resistance shall
Make landing ere the cruel First Order doth.
May it be so, else all is lost indeed.

Enter POE DAMERON.

No sooner is it spoken than 'tis done.
Our hope arriveth in this pilot's form.   30

POE   Good Master Tekka, we have heard it told
You do have knowledge as may bring us aid:
Where we may find the Jedi Skywalker.
For though the mighty man hath flown away,
And whether 'twas in night, or in a day,   35
Or in a vision or, mayhap, in none,
Is he, therefore, still any the less gone?

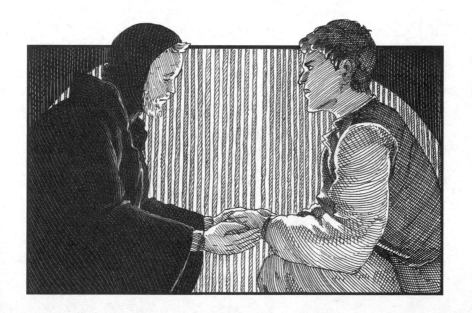

LOR   Our time draws short, e'en as thou askest this.
      I bid thee, take this storage unit here,
      Which I for many years have safe preserv'd: 40
      It shall begin to set all things aright.
      My travels o'er the wayward galaxy
      Have taken me too far, most verily.
      Mine eyes have seen far more than any orbs
      Should witness of misfortune and despair.   45
      Without the Jedi, balance there is none
      Within the Force.

POE   —That motley drama, O,
      Be sure, it shall not be forgot! And now,
      Our chance anon shall be reality.
      The general tenaciously hath search'd   50
      For this intelligence for length of days.

LOR   The general—O, appellation strange!
      My mind and heart do claim her royalty.

POE   Heav'n have her in its sacred keep! She is.

Enter BB-8.

BB-8   Zzwaflit blee roohblic bleeflib zilf blikflii,   55
      Blox flirzooz blis blox flitblic bloozood flir
      Reej zoodreej blee reej flirblip zzwaflit flirr
      Bluuflir zoonflii flew blavrooq bleeflit blis!

POE   Lo! Death hath rear'd himself a throne and doth
      Approach with haste. We shall have company,   60
      Thus you must hide.

LOR   —And thou, my lad, must leave.
      Get hence! Deliver my fond hope to her.

                                    [Exit Lor.

Enter a mighty battalion of STORMTROOPERS,
including CAPTAIN PHASMA *and* FN-2187.
Enter several CITIZENS OF JAKKU *severally, fighting in opposition.*

POE   Roll swiftly as thou canst, good BB-8—
               Kind solace in a dying hour thou art!
BB-8   Flip flli zzwablic zilf blooblee zoom reej blee!   65
                              [*Poe and BB-8 climb into Poe's X-wing*
                                  starfighter. Stormtroopers fire at his ship.
POE   This wreck—this ruin—O, these stones, alas!
               My ship is struck with harsh and searing blows
               That may, methinks, mean devastation soon.
BB-8   Flewflit blay rooh zzwa bleezilf blayflit zood
               Flip blooflib blic flig bloorooh zoom blip blee.   70
POE   Thanks, kindly BB-8, I see them come,
               And shall respond with fire to take their lives!
                              [*Poe returns fire on the stormtroopers and then*
                                          exits his damaged ship.
               The hardest day, the hardest hour mine eyes
               Shall see—have ever seen! The ship is sack'd,
               And I'll not leave here but as prisoner.   75
               'Tis certain so, I see the battle's end.
               I therefore shall entrust unto my droid
               The storage unit Lor hath given me.
               I prithee, BB-8, attend me now!
               Take thou this databank, for it shall be   80
               Far more secure in thy care than in mine.
                              [*Poe places the data storage unit inside BB-8.*
               Now get thee gone as far as thou canst roll.
               Dost thou attend?
BB-8   —Flip blayblee bleezoom zzwa.

POE   At morn—at noon—at twilight dim—whene'er
                   The time arriveth, I shall come for thee.   85
                                            [*Exit BB-8.*
                   What stand against these foes may one man make?
                   I am outnumber'd hundreds to my one.
                   Still, I will make whatever fight I can,
                   And mayhap freedom shall be my reward.
                        [*Across the stage, FN-2187's comrade FN-2003*
                              is slain while FN-2187 kneels nearby.

FN-2187   Alas, thou fallen stormtrooper and friend—   90
                   FN-2003, my squadmate true.
                   Thou diest on this battlefield, e'en here,
                   The first engagement in which I have fought.
                   Like womp rats in a nest we were fix'd fast
                   As we flew in the transport to Jakku.   95
                   Form'd into order'd, stately rows of white,
                   Prepar'd for years for battle on this night.
                   Each one of us a soldier, train'd and skill'd,
                   Ta'en from our families and rais'd to kill.
                   The great First Order is our only kin,   100
                   Our chieftains hold the claim to parentage,
                   For we know naught of ties of family—
                   Our squadron is our first community.
                   Yet here, this night wherein I come to fight,
                   I find myself dismay'd by horrid sights: 105
                   My comrade bloody, fallen, dead, and gone,
                   As we make slaughter of these innocents.
                   I cannot fight—my mind hath shaken loose
                   Of what the strong First Order doth require.

Enter KYLO REN *in his shuttle.*

POE   What is this ship that draweth quickly near,   110
            Intimidating in its entrance grim?
            O, it doth shake the very heav'n on high
            With tumult as it thunders by so bleak.
            'Tis likely that some fiend doth ride therein—
            A dark apostle of the foul First Order.   115

                                   [Poe hides.

Enter STORMTROOPERS *escorting* LOR SAN TEKKA, *who is
in custody. They bring him before* KYLO REN.

KYLO   Mine entrance is the very knell of death,
            Which doth come ringing for mine enemies.
            Disciple of the dark side, Kylo Ren,
            So am I now and evermore shall be.
            My weaker past behind me, I am here   120
            To show the reach of the First Order's might.
            Tonight begins our govern ultimate.
            Not gone, defeated or forgotten, nay,
            For with the Jedi ended, we shall be
            Unbreakable, alive, and damn all else.   125
            [*To Lor:*] Behold, thou knave, how old thou art
                                   become.

LOR   'Tis not so pitiful and tragic as
            The loathsome fate that hath befallen thee.

KYLO   Thou knowest what my presence here requires—
            The thing for which I seek, pray make it plain.   130
            I'll not abide your parries and your jests,
            No trick shall thwart the will of Kylo Ren.

LOR   What thou hast come for is not my concern;
                'Tis whence thou comest that I know full well,
                The time ere thou didst claim the name of Ren.   135

KYLO   The map to the rank Jedi Skywalker:
                We know thou has discover'd it at last.
                Thou shalt to the First Order give this map.

LOR   The base First Order from the dark side rose,
                Yet thou didst not.

KYLO   —The dark side thou shalt see,   140
                For I shall show its deadly power to thee.

LOR   Belike thou shalt endeavor so to do.
                Still, thou canst not deny the simple truth:
                The family whence thou hast come.

KYLO   —Indeed.

                  [Kylo Ren slays Lor San Tekka.

POE   He was a goodly spirit—he who fell.   145
                I shall take my revenge whilst time permits.

                [Poe reveals himself, firing at Kylo Ren.
                Kylo Ren uses the Force to stop the blast short
                and freeze Poe. Stormtroopers bring Poe
                to Kylo Ren.

                What happens next, O friend and fiend of hell?
                'Tis I shall speak, or you, or what you will?
                Pray speak, Count, 'tis your cue.

KYLO   —The old man hath
                Giv'n what I seek to thee, Resistance scum.   150

POE   Most difficult it is to hear your words
                Withal the apparatus that doth mire
                Your visage from my sight. The night, though clear,
                Shall frown, and all the stars shall not look down
                Upon your hidden and most hideous face,   155

Most cowardly enwrapp'd in that black mask.
What is it that doth make a man like you
Make haste to hide himself from others' sight?
Are you afeard your deeds shall be made known?
Or do you think, observing not your eyes,   160
I shall not know the evil in your heart?

KYLO   [to Trooper 1:] Search thou this man.

TROOPER 1   —He nothing hath, my
                                                    lord.

KYLO   Deposit this weak rogue aboard my ship—
              His veilèd secrets shall not long be kept.
                    [Stormtroopers strike Poe and carry him away.
                    Captain Phasma approaches Kylo Ren.

PHASMA   Sir, what of all the villagers herein,   165
              Who have borne witness to our fierce attack?
              What is your iron will, as touching them?

KYLO   Destroy them all—not even one shall live.

PHASMA   [to stormtroopers:] At my command, do steel your
                                        nerves and fire!
                    [The stormtroopers fire at the villagers.

FN-2187   [aside:] O, vicious deed! Unspeakable and foul, 170
              Fie! Evil goes uncheck'd, soars limitless,
              And fury, wrath, and death have ta'en the day.
              I shall not fire my weapon, come what will—
              Damn'd be the consequence for mine inaction,
              For now to act would be my soul to slay.   175

KYLO   [aside:] I sense a stormtrooper who doth not shoot—
              Whose conscience, mayhap, speaks to him with lies.
              This shall I both recall and contemplate,
              Lest to some future ill it doth translate.
                                                    [Exeunt.

SCENE 2.
Aboard the Finalizer.

Enter POE DAMERON, *guarded by* STORMTROOPERS.
Enter FN-2187 *severally.*

POE   I have been ta'en unto a station vast,
               Existence whereof the Resistance knows
               But little and suspects e'en less. 'Tis plain
               The base First Order groweth quick and strong.
               Behold the ships within this stronghold grim,   5
               Arrang'd for battle and destruction swift.
               My mind begins to tremble at this sight,
               And fear—which doth betray my better sense—
               Hath stirr'd from out th'abysses of my heart.
                              [Exeunt Poe and stormtroopers.
FN-2187   [*removing his helmet:*] My mind still reels from what
                              mine eyes did see   10
               Upon the dreadful planet of Jakku.
               'Tis certain that the planet's curs'd by Fate,
               And if I ne'er return unto its surface
               'Twill yet be all too soon for such as I.

                    Enter CAPTAIN PHASMA.

PHASMA   FN-2187, show thy mettle—   15
               Thou shalt submit thy blaster for inspection.
FN-2187   Forsooth, my captain, e'en as you do say.
PHASMA   And is thy brain chang'd into worthless scrap?
               Who is the officer superior

Who hath giv'n their permission for the odd   20
Removal of thy helmet from thy head?
FN-2187   Apologies, fair captain. None was giv'n.
PHASMA   Pray, mine thy heart for true obedience,
            And make report to my division soon.
                                              [*Exit Captain Phasma.*

FN-2187   O, now sit still, my soul. Foul deeds will rise,   25
            Though all of life o'erwhelm them, to mine eyes.
                                              [*Exit FN-2187.*

SCENE 3.

On the planet Jakku.

Enter REY. *Enter* UNKAR PLUTT *aside, in an outpost stall.*

REY   Pull'd by a longing deep within my soul,
            Each day I struggle merely to endure:
            Repeating mine endeavors day by day,
            Content to wait for those I know shall come.
            Here on Jakku, I make my simple way: 5
            Among the junkyards I go scavenging,
            Not to discover aught of treasure, nay—
            Collecting merely remnants, bits and scraps,
            Enow to earn the food that keeps me whole.
            I climb within the mighty fallen crafts,   10
            A'scrambing o'er a starship's inward parts.
            My body able, fit for such a task,
            Strong both in sinew and in mind am I—
            Of more than just a scrounger's heart possess'd.
            Methinks it is a solitary life,   15

E'er looking to the skies or to the stars
And hoping for my dear ones who did leave—
Now long ago—to make their homecoming.
Continually do I yearn for them,
E'en as I spend my hours in toil and want.   20
Still, there is plenty here to fill my time:
The careful ravage of the *Ravager*—
One of the many ships through which I seek—
Revisiting the wreckage ev'ry day,
Observing some new salvageable piece.   25
Requiring patience, care, and bravery,
Collecting junk from starships is my lot.
Hours pass, until 'tis time to leave the ruins;
I make descent with newfound parts, and then
Load them upon my trusted sliding sand board.   30
Departing quick atop my speeder swift,
O'er all the dunes, past rank steelpecker birds,
Fly I across the barren wilderness.
Hie then to Niima Outpost with my wares,
I drag my sand board 'cross the golden silt.   35
My things I polish with the utmost care—
There seated near the older scroungers, who
Have spent their lives entire in drudgery—
E'en there I scrub the junk with wearied hopes.
Fate hath, it seems, no other thread for me.   40
At last, I go to junk boss Unkar Plutt,
Baseborn and rude, a scoundrel full of greed.
Looks he upon the scraps I have discover'd,
E'er cheating me a little more each day,
Decides he, then, what paltry sum he'll proffer.   45
Jakku is not a planet for the weak,

Especially for those who shrink in fear.
Determination is the only virtue
I've found to be a safeguard in this place.
One who hath vigor, wit, and fortitude,   50
Belike shall be the one who doth prevail.
In past times, I believ'd I'd not survive.
With age comes strength, with strength comes
                                    perseverance,
And thus I persevere. Pray, know my name:
Nearby, the sun shines bright; I am its Rey.   55
             [Rey approaches Unkar Plutt and
                    hands him her junk scraps.

UNKAR   What thou hast brought me here today is worth
         One quarter portion.

REY   —Thus it swiftly goes:
         They'll hate who shall, while I must shake it off.
                              [Exit Unkar.

Back to my humble shelter I return,
Inside a walker of Imperial times.   60
The portion giv'n to me by Unkar Plutt
Becometh that on which I dine by sunset.
Veg-meat and polystarch have little taste,
Yet shall maintain my health as I have need.
I shall be seated on the sandy ground,   65
And take my meal whilst donning this gray helmet,
Which once a warrior did proudly wear,
Who now is but a hidden skull and bones.
Another dusk hath fallen on Jakku—
I'll mark the time with scratch upon the wall   70
As I have done for many thousand days:
The record of mine isolation here,

Each line a blemish on my youthful soul.

Enter BB-8 *aside, in a net pulled*
by TEEDO *riding astride a* LUGGABEAST.

BB-8	Blav blicflir bleeflib zzwa flit blisblox blee,
	Flliblik roohzoon zooz zzwaflew blav zoom blee! 75
REY	[*to Teedo:*] Talama parqua!
TEEDO	—Da—bee da padoo!
REY	Nadan ta parqua!

[Rey begins to cut BB-8 free from the net.

TEEDO	—Nee, dee yan, duh rookah.
REY	Huh nomah!
TEEDO	—Reeya boonja bonganoo.

[Exit Teedo.

BB-8	Blik flli blayblis roohzilf roil bloozzwa blee?
REY	'Twas no more than one Teedo, he most vile, 80
	Who wants to take thee for thine inward parts.
	He hath respect for naught and no one, nay.
	Come, let me look on thee, for I can see
	Thou hast a bent antenna. Come, I prithee.

[Rey fixes BB-8's antenna.

	Whence hast thou ventur'd to Jakku, my friend? 85
BB-8	Flewzzwa zoodrooh, bluuflit blav flliblox blis
	Zoomblic bluuroil zooz zzwa flewblis blay blis
	Flig flliflig zilfflir flliflit blee blavzood.
REY	'Tis classified, indeed? Ah, me as well.
	A most profound and well-kept secret, I: 90
	Mysterious unto the last—ha! Nay,
	A secret is but secret if there is
	Another soul within the galaxy

Who'd care to know it. I am too alone
To be wrapp'd up in secrets, verily.   95
But there's an end with talk of secrets: if
Thou roll'st thyself most spherical in that
Direction, Niima Outpost thou shalt find.
Yet, be forewarn'd: go not near Kelvin Ridge,
And stay far from the northern sinking fields,   100
Lest thou mayst drown within a sandy tomb.

BB-8   Blox flliblik zood zoozflig rooqbloo zoonflew
              Blip flliblox flit bluu roohblis flitzilf rooh
              Blav bleeflir blee.

REY   —Nay, follow not with me.
              Thou must go thither if thou'd reach the town.   105

BB-8   Zoom blisblik flit rooqzzwa blooblay rooq flew
              Reej flliblav flitflig roohzoom zoomzoon blee,

	Zooz flli flitblip rooqflir zoonzzwa flew blay.	
REY	O, follow, then.	
BB-8	—Zoomreej bluubloo flewblay!	
REY	Yet in the morning thou must go away,	110
	For ample struggle have I in this place	
	To keep myself alive, much less a droid—	
	E'en such an amiable droid as thou.	
BB-8	Bloozoom blavblay bloxflit rooq roohblip zzwa	
	Reejzoon zilfblok bleeblis.	
REY	—Thou welcome art.	115

        [*Aside:*] This droidly friend I had not hop'd to find,
        Yet presently our two fates are entwin'd.

                [Exeunt, traveling to Rey's shelter.

SCENE 4.

Aboard the Finalizer.

Enter KYLO REN *on balcony.* POE DAMERON *is aside, also on balcony, unconscious and bound to an interrogation chair.*

KYLO	The dark side is the calling I embrace,	
	For 'tis the heritage I have receiv'd:	
	To bring the final Jedi to disgrace.	
	The Knights of Ren did first give me my place,	
	And in their care my gifts were first conceiv'd—	5
	The dark side is the calling I embrace.	
	Luke Skywalker's last steps my mind shall trace	
	Until, at last, his capture is achiev'd	
	To bring the final Jedi to disgrace.	
	Thus I'll interrogate this pilot base,	10

Until the information is retriev'd;
The dark side is the calling I embrace.
And when, at last, Skywalker I outpace,
The dark side's strength by all shall be perceiv'd—
To bring the final Jedi to disgrace.   15
Thus let the interview proceed apace—
Mine expectation shall not be aggriev'd.
The dark side is the calling I embrace,
To bring the final Jedi to disgrace.
                    [Kylo Ren approaches Poe, who awakens.

POE   You nevermore shall win, you villain vile.   20
KYLO   I did not know the bravest pilot of
           The small Resistance was aboard our ship.
           Art thou most comfortable, Resistance brute?
POE   O, evil thing in robe of sorrow, nay.
KYLO   Thou hast impress'd me by thy seeming might: 25
           Though we have tried, none yet hath broken thee,
           Or pick'd the lock of thy most fasten'd mind
           To find what thou hast done with th'map we seek.
POE   Your keys and other instruments have fail'd,
           For I am not a door that may be open'd,   30
           Or trunk that holds a mystery for you.
           Where I have kept that secret, none shall know,
           And thus my hidden mem'ry is to me
           Like some enchanted far-off isle in some
           Tumultuous sea, where you cannot reach.   35
KYLO   [aside:] Now come, O dark side of the Force severe,
           And move within me to unbolt his mind.
                         [Kylo Ren uses the Force to try to extract
                                    thoughts from Poe's mind.
           [To Poe:] Where is it? I will know, and shall, indeed.

POE   Let your heart from its present pathway part!
              The brave Resistance shall not be coerc'd: 40
              Intimidation shall not break our will.
KYLO   Where is it? Thou shalt tell me.
POE   —O, alas!
              Would I could wake—my soul is sorely shaken!
                     [Poe screams as Kylo Ren overcomes
                                    his resistance to the Force.

                     Enter GENERAL HUX, *on balcony.*

KYLO   [*to Hux:*] The map is in a droid, upon Jakku,
              Within a BB unit.
HUX   —Very well,   45
              Our troops shall have it soon within our grasp.
KYLO   Pray, make it so. 'Tis now within your care.
              Yea, Luke Skywalker shall escape us ne'er.
                                                    [Exeunt.

SCENE 5.
On the planet Jakku.

Enter REY *and* BB-8. *Enter* UNKAR PLUTT *aside, in an outpost stall.*

REY   Whate'er thou do, make sure thou keep'st thy hope,
              For 'tis what shall sustain thee on Jakku.
              Whoe'er thou waitest on may yet appear,
              O droid call'd Classified. Believe thou me,
              When waiting is the subject, I am master.   5
BB-8   Blox flewblic rooh reej blooblay flli flirblis

Zoon blit zoozblit blip roohblik blooblox bluu
Blay flewflib zzwaroil flli roohflit bluublee
Reejblis zoonflit rooq zilf flit blooblox flir?

REY   My family are they whom I expect;   10
They shall return one day, I know 'tis true.
Come with me now, we must to Unkar Plutt.
                 [Rey and BB-8 approach Unkar Plutt,
                     and Rey hands him her junk scraps.

UNKAR   These pieces five, by mine own reckoning,
Are worth a mere half portion.

REY   —What? Thou knave!
Last week they were worth half a portion each;   15
Belike the sum should be two and a half.
And now thou sayest 'tis one half alone?
Is junk so plentiful upon Jakku
That 'tis no longer valuable to thee?
Can junk make decrease or increase in value,   20
For still it is but junk. It this not so?

UNKAR   Enough of prating: say, what of thy droid?
REY   What of him, eh?
UNKAR   —I shall pay thee for him.
Full sixty portions he is worth to me.

REY   *[aside:]* O, riches I have ne'er imaginèd!   25
This vast amount would feed me for a year.
Yet look at this poor droid, so innocent
And clearly with a mission on his mind.
If I abandon him to Unkar Plutt,
'Twould be no better than when I was small   30
And felt bereft by mine own family.
O, give me strength: I must reject this deal.
[To Unkar:] I shall decline; the droid is not for sale.

Come, BB-8, let us withdraw anon.
                              [Exeunt Rey and BB-8.

UNKAR   [*into communicator:*] I bid thee, though it seemeth
                                        paranoid, 35
Pray follow her and bring me back the droid.
                                        [Exit.

SCENE 6.

Aboard the Finalizer *and on the planet Jakku.*

Enter FN-2187.

FN-2187   My mind hath been decided, finally,
               Though far too long I've thought on this decision.
               I shall escape the harsh First Order soon,
               And shall the netted pilot fly withal.
               Between his skill and mine own uniform,   5
               We have the things we need to flee this place.

Enter a STORMTROOPER *with* POE DAMERON, *who is bound.*

               [*To trooper:*] Ren swiftly would receive the prisoner.
               Unbind the fiend; I shall escort him thither.
                              [The stormtrooper unbinds Poe and exits.
               I prithee, hear my words anon, good fellow:
               If thou wilt listen, I shall help thee flee.   10
POE   What dost thou mean? If I hear thee aright,
               Thy words do fall like starlight on a pall.
FN-2187   Herein doth lie a rescue: follow'st thou?
               Hast thou the talent TIE fighters to fly?

POE   Thou art an emblem of the glow of hope.   15
              Art thou with the Resistance, sirrah kind?
FN-2187   Nay, nay, I merely am thy ticket off.
              Canst thou, I prithee, fly TIE fighters?
POE   —Aye.
              There is no vessel that hath bested me,
              For I can pilot anything that flies.   20
              But wherefore art thou helping me, my friend?
              How many thoughts of what entombèd hopes
              I dar'd to dream, but near had given up.
FN-2187   'Tis but the fair and noble thing to do.
POE   Forever changing places, by my troth!   25
              Thou dost a pilot need, my friend. 'Tis true?
FN-2187   Forsooth, I need a pilot.
POE   —This shall be.
              I'd go with thee in sunshine and in shadow.

          Enter many STORMTROOPERS *and* GUARDS *as* FN-2187 *and*
             POE DAMERON *proceed to the* Finalizer's *main hangar.*

FN-2187   O, be thou calm, ne'er fearful. O, be calm!
POE   I am most calm. My heart is brighter than   30
              The many stars within the sky above.
FN-2187   I am but speaking to myself, not thee.
              Now here, fall speedily aside with me!
                     [FN-2187 and Poe step quickly aside, into a
                        waiting TIE fighter. They enter its cabin.
POE   Long have I wish'd to fly one of these ships:
              Twin ion engines, legendary TIE,   35
              The mystery which binds me still in awe!
              Tell me, my newfound comrade, canst thou shoot?

FN-2187	Of blasters, certainly, I know full well.
POE	The principle's the same within this ship.
	The toggle thou shalt find upon the left 40
	Can switch 'twixt cannons, missiles, and mag pulse.
	The sight's upon the right wherewith thou aim'st,
	And use the trigger for to fire. Dost see?
	Pray let thy heart be light, upraise no dirge!
FN-2187	O, complicated system of controls! 45

> [They begin to take off but are stopped by a
> cable attached to the TIE fighter.

POE	Alack! Yet I shall clear this snag forthwith.
	Our star dials all are pointed to the morn—
	We two shall steer their course and fly anon!

Enter COLONEL KAPLAN *and* OFFICER THANISSON *above, on balcony.*

THANISSON	I'd not believe it, yet mine eyes do see:
	Unsanction'd, a departure from bay two! 50
KAPLAN	Alert the general, e'en Hux, and stop
	That fighter from departing from the ship!

> [Exeunt Colonel Kaplan and
> Officer Thannison. Stormtroopers
> begin shooting at the TIE fighter.
> FN-2187 takes the controls and fires back.

FN-2187	Though ye have been my friends and comrades both,
	You shall not stand athwart my passage. Fie!
POE	We have escap'd, and fly among the stars 55
	Like some full-orbèd moon that, like a soul,
	Sought a precipitate pathway through heav'n.

> [Exeunt stormtroopers as
> Poe and FN-2187 fly into space.

O, how this vessel soars most pow'rfully!
See thou those cannons yon? Thou must destroy
Them utterly, lest they do us destroy;   60
We shall not venture far if they are whole.
I shall put us into position, thou
Give ev'ry gun thy sight but few thy shot.
Ahead, ahead, dost see? A target clean,
If thou canst hit it.

               [FN-2187 shoots and destroys the cannon.

FN-2187   —Ay, I shall not fail!   65
Didst thou see? Ha! My finest shot! Didst see?

POE   I saw, forsooth. Thy hearty, joyous laugh
Is like the tintinnabulation that
So musically wells up from the spheres!
What is thy name, O worthy rescuer?   70

FN-2187   FN-2187 is my name.
It is the only name that was for me,
The only name the vile First Order gave,
The only name, forc'd on me by cruel men,
The only name—of signs and numbers form'd.   75

POE   I shall not use the letter-digit phrase
By which a hateful enemy hath call'd
Thee, soldier, utterly expendable.
Say, what of Finn? How doth this title suit?
By that dear name I e'er shall call on thee,   80
Thou who art more than brother unto me.

FINN   Finn. Finn! Indeed, it suits me well, my friend.
I'll be the quickest Finn that e'er did steer
The brawny figure of a colo claw,
The fish that swimmeth 'neath the briny depths!   85

POE   My name is Poe—Poe Dameron am I.

	We shall be friends: 'tis well to know thee, sirrah.	
	A voice from out the future cries, "On! On!"	
	We shall be friends whate'er the episode.	
FINN	'Tis well to know thee too, my new friend, Poe.	90

> *Enter* KYLO REN, GENERAL HUX, *and an*
> OFFICER *above, on balcony.*

OFFICER	They have destroy'd the turbo lasers, sir.	
HUX	I prithee, use the ventral cannons, then.	
OFFICER	Ay, sir, we shall anon bring them online.	
KYLO	Good general, is't the Resistance pilot?	
	Hath he somehow absconded?	
HUX	—Verily,	95
	And had he help, from one of our own men.	
	E'en now we search the registers to find	
	The traitorous stormtrooper who did aid him.	
KYLO	The Force doth know what your computers seek:	
	'Twas that one from the village on Jakku:	100
	FN-2187. Fie upon't!	
OFFICER	The ventral cannon is prepar'd to strike.	
HUX	Fire thou with all the fury thou canst send.	
	We'll spill the blood that hath today escap'd!	
	[Exeunt Kylo Ren, General Hux, and officer.	
POE	One shot approacheth hastily. Dost see?	105
	My right is right, thy left is also right.	
	How statue-like I see thee stand—be brave!	
	[Finn shoots one cannon.	
	Well aim'd, we may evade this salvo yet!	
FINN	Yet wait, where are we bound? Where fliest thou?	
POE	E'en by a route obscure and lonely must	110

	We swiftly make return unto Jakku.
FINN	Back to Jakku? Our newfound friendship hits
	Its first blockade. Nay, not unto Jakku—
	We must depart the system sans deferment!
POE	My droid must be retriev'd ere the First Order

         We swiftly make return unto Jakku.

FINN   Back to Jakku? Our newfound friendship hits
Its first blockade. Nay, not unto Jakku—
We must depart the system sans deferment!

POE   My droid must be retriev'd ere the First Order   115
Takes him into captivity. He is
The truest—the most fervently devoted.
A BB unit, white with orange, too.
He hath no peer in all the galaxy.

FINN   His color doth concern me not, fair Poe,   120
But mine own color if we do not leave:
The yellow of the fearfulness I feel,
The blue of my heart, frozen in my chest,
The red blood that shall fall when I am dead.
No droid could be so vital to our fates.   125
It is unfathomable—we must leave,
Put the First Order far behind us. See?
If we return, our sentence sure is death.

POE   My sentence is: we shall find BB-8.
The droid is trusting to the mild-eyed stars,   130
And holdeth he a map to Luke Skywalker!

FINN   This far-gone droid withal thou art consum'd!
Pray tell me, friend, that thou dost only jest.

                [The TIE fighter is blasted by a
                cannon shot. Exit Poe. Finn falls to
                the surface of Jakku in the ship.

        Enter GENERAL HUX, CAPTAIN PHASMA, *and*
        OFFICER UNAMO *above, on balcony.*

PHASMA   FN-2187 made report

| | Unto mine own division. There was he | 135 |

Unto mine own division. There was he   135
Evaluated carefully and sent
To have his courage solder'd up and to
Be recondition'd, for to serve again.

HUX   Show'd he e'er signs of nonconformity?

PHASMA   This was his first offense, and first I saw   140
Of his deep feebleness, as weak as tin.

UNAMO   My general, their vessel hath been hit.

HUX   Destroy'd?

UNAMO   —Disabl'd, bound unto Jakku.
The fighter shall make landing in the badlands
Of Goazan.

HUX   —Back for the droid, no doubt.   145
With haste dispatch a squad unto the wreckage!

                    [Exeunt General Hux, Captain Phasma,
                              and Officer Unamo.

FINN   What's this? Alone upon a lifeless dune.
Yet where is Poe? O, Poe, where hast thou fall'n?

                    [Finn searches around the wrecked TIE fighter.
                         He finds Poe's doublet and picks it up.

The fighter's here, yet pilot is there none.
His doublet only is what's left of him.   150
The man hath flown away, sans trace or hint.
Yea, disappear'd, an 'twere a fairy tale.

                    [The ground under Finn begins to shake.

The ground doth shake! Is failure not enow?
Shall ev'ry element turn foe as well?

                    [Finn steps away from the TIE fighter.
                    The sinking sands swallow the fighter whole.

Fie! Wonder 'fore mine eyes, most horrible!   155
Was Poe made landlord of a sandy grave?

Did he attend a desert funeral?
Do his bones lie full fathom five below,
His final resting place upon the dune?
O, may it not be so, yet so I fear.   160
The man belike is dead: mine only friend.
What shall I do? I have borne fardels plenty,
And now—for Poe, and for myself—must live.
                    [Finn begins walking away from
                    the wreckage, removing his uniform
                    and donning Poe's doublet.
My stormtrooper veneer I do forsake,
And make my life hereafter as a man: 165
The odious First Order I disown,
And shall, from now, with honor mark my days.
Too long I play'd my cards and bet my life—
I wager'd, like a fool, with mine own soul.
The future look'd as bright as any diamond,   170
But wretched duty form'd a knocking club
That furnish'd me with only crooked spades,
With which I might forfend my weary heart.
The mean First Order held the final card—
The trump that would undo me finally.   175
This trump card was my freedom's shocking end,
The king that did make forfeit all my days,
This card did lie to me and all my friends,
This trump was base and fickle, villainous.
The cruel First Order conn'd me from the first,   180
And rais'd me to be faithful to its ends—
I was confin'd to years of losing bets.
My life was play'd away e'en from my birth,
The ante that I ow'd too great a fine

Than I could pay had I five hundred lives.   185
When man is but a number, standing fix'd
Against a foe that's far more powerful,
He'll fail at ev'ry trick and hand and game.
Thus I shall leave my life of cards behind,
No more to gamble in a game of folly,   190
Wherein the stakes are far too high for me.
My life ere now was but a prelude to
The future, which I do embrace with yearning.
But soft, what is this vision that appears?
Far off I see a post where I'll begin   195
My life anew: no trooper I, but Finn.

[Exit.

SCENE 1.

Aboard the Finalizer.

Enter GENERAL HUX *and* KYLO REN.

HUX Our Supreme Leader Snoke explicit was:
Detain the droid if we've the wherewithal,
Destroy it if we must.

KYLO —How capable
Are these, your soldiers, whom we send to do't?

HUX My methods shall not answer to your queries. 5

KYLO 'Tis certain you have no objection to
Committing e'en the highest treason, hmm?
Perhaps our leader Snoke would benefit
From clone-led army, rather than your troops.

HUX My soldiers are exceptionally train'd, 10
Programm'd from birth, ere they do parents know,
To serve, to heed, to fight, and to obey.

KYLO They should, therefore, have little trouble with
This mission on Jakku—retrieve the droid,
Sans its destruction. Do you understand? 15

HUX Take care, dark Ren, that purpose personal
Doth not our leader Snoke's will contradict.

KYLO I want the map, and have it soon I shall.
For your sake, pray deliver it anon.

                              [*Exit Kylo Ren.*

HUX Oh, how that man doth stir my very soul— 20
A young man, yea, yet still a valid threat.
His power with the dark side hath increas'd
Beyond what I can fathom or imagine.

He, though, should render me the due respect
That doth befit the title General: 25
I am no juvenile, naïve recruit,
No beastly soldier of the lowest rank.
I am no less than Hux, the general,
And should be giv'n the proper deference.
Yet Kylo Ren by other thoughts is mov'd,   30
Not soon impress'd by title, place, or rank—
He hath no dread of his superiors
Save Snoke, who causes all to be afeard.
Thus, if to gain my leader Snoke's esteem
I must discover and bring back the droid,   35
I shall do it, with ev'ry mean employ'd.

                                                              [Exit.

SCENE 2.

On the planet Jakku, at Niima Outpost.

Enter FINN. *Enter a* HAPPABORE *aside, drinking from a trough.*

FINN   Lo, I have walk'd five hundred miles at least,
            And I would walk five hundred more, forsooth!
            Nay, not five hundred, mayhap four or five—
            Sufficient distance, still, to work me woe.
            O, now my throat is parch'd, on fire with thirst,   5
            And only water satisfies its burn.
            Yet in this awful outpost is the taste
            Of water an exclusive luxury.
            I am not proud, not Finn, not in this life:
            There stands a fierce and mighty happabore   10

Who drinks his fill of water from the trough—
I'll thither haply, for to quench my thirst.
                    [Finn runs to the happabore's
                    watering hole and drinks greedily.
O, water foul, yet sweet upon my lips!

HAPPABORE [*aside:*] O, wherefore should it be that I am call'd
A beast of burthen, when my burthen is   15
To share my water with an animal
Far wilder, more voracious, than myself?
He hath the look of madness in his eyes,
Whilst I am an enlighten'd happabore:
I do my work upon Jakku's bleak dunes,   20
As any must, who would survive this clime.
Thereafter, though, when day hath turn'd to night,
I make my way unto my shelter meek,
And read the classic tales that are renown'd

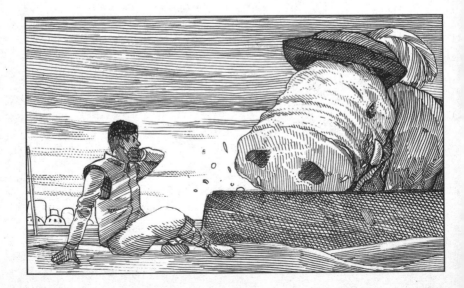

Throughout our galaxy: my mind is sharp   25
Though some may think my body base and rude.
Give me a book to read, a mind to think,
And time to contemplate life's mysteries,
And ye shall find a happy happabore—
Far more refin'd than th'man who drinketh here.   30
                                        [Exit happabore.

Enter REY, *surrounded by and fighting*
with two RUFFIANS. *Enter* BB-8, *behind.*

FINN   What's this, a maid in danger? Fie upon't!
            I shall a feat of bravery endeavor!
                    [Rey fights off the ruffians, who exit hastily.
            The lady is formidable, indeed,
            No freeing doth she need, to my chagrin.
            But soft, the droid who with her stands—is it   35
            The BB unit whereof Poe did speak?
BB-8   [*to Rey, seeing Finn:*] Bluuzoom zood blayflig zoomflit
                                        zzwablic blis
            Blip flitflew blee roohflir bluublis blip reej
            Blox zzwablis blic zoozblik blooblee roilflit!
REY   'Tis he! Avaunt, thou scurvy, wretched knave!   40
                            [Rey begins chasing Finn.
FINN   From hero unto harried in a trice!
                    [Finn is caught and leveled by Rey's quarterstaff.
REY   Where art thou bound, thou vile, conniving thief?
FINN   Thief? [*BB-8 shocks Finn.*] O, alas! Now wherefore
                                        shock'st thou me?
REY   The pilot's doublet wherewith thou art cloth'd—
            The droid hath told me it is stolen. Was't?   45

FINN   This day hath been an 'twere a lifetime whole;
              Thy patience and forbearance I would have.
                              [BB-8 shocks Finn again.
              Wilt thou, I prithee, end thy fearful pricks?

REY   Where didst thou find the doublet? For the droid
              Doth say it was his master's property.   50

FINN   Faith, 'twas the doublet of Poe Dameron.
              That is his name? Thy master and thy chief?
              The rank First Order captur'd him, and I
              Did help him hither flee, unto Jakku.
              Our small TIE fighter, though, did crash nearby.   55
              Unfortunately, Poe hath flown his last,
              For he is dead and gone beneath the dunes.
              I fain would save him; my condolences.

BB-8   Flib zzwablic roilzoon zzwa zood blicflit blik.
                              [BB-8 rolls aside in grief.

REY   Thou art, therefore, with the Resistance strong?   60

FINN   [aside:] She now regards me with a lofty eye!
              I'd not her heart extinguish, all aflame.
              [To Rey:] Forsooth, I am Resistance in itself.
              A pilot of the bold Resistance, yea,
              Resistance is my faith, my suit, my hope,   65
              And of Resistance am I finely made.

REY   O, wondrous soul! Ere now the face of the
              Resistance I have ne'er laid eyes upon.

FINN   We fighters of the valiant Resistance
              All look like me—or else look different.   70

REY   The droid, this BB-8, doth tell the tale
              Of secret missions and the hidden base
              To which he must return with all due haste.

FINN   Thus Poe hath spoken, too, for BB-8

	Doth hold a map to find Luke Skywalker.	75
	It seemeth friend and foe alike do seek't.	
REY	Luke Skywalker, e'en he? Methought 'twas myth,	
	A bedtime tale to whisper to the young.	

Enter STORMTROOPERS.
BB-8 *rolls toward* REY *and* FINN *in haste.*

BB-8	Zzwaflit blipflir bleebloo flew blooblox blip	
	Roohblis bleeblic zoon bloobluu zoombluu blee!	80
FINN	Stormtroopers do approach—hold fast my hand!	

*[Finn takes Rey by the hand and starts
running away. BB-8 follows them.*

REY	Hast thou gone mad? Why pullest thou mine hand?	
FINN	I bid thee, fly, there is no time to talk!	
	Flee, BB-8, anon!	
REY	—Pray, let me go!	
	Unhand me, by my troth. [*To BB-8:*] Stay close, good	
	droid!	85
	Come by this route—I know where we must go.	
TROOPER 1	[*to Trooper 2:*] Call in the air strike; they shall not	
	escape!	
REY	[*to Finn:*] They shoot at both of us, not merely thee.	
FINN	They did find thee with me, thus art thou mark'd.	
REY	My thanks for that. I askèd not for this.	90
FINN	'Twas not I who pursu'd thee with a staff!	
	Hath no one blasters in this awful place?	
REY	Sweet BB-8, art thou in good repair?	
BB-8	Blav flli zilfrooh flew bleezoom zzwa blavflir	
	Blayblis bloxrooh flit fllibloo blip blay blis!	95
FINN	The sound of ships a'flying through the air!	

[*Finn takes Rey's hand again and pulls her*
away, running. BB-8 follows behind.

Enter TIE FIGHTERS *of the First Order.*

REY   Release my hand—I need not thy protection!
I swear, the next time thou dost take my hand,
Thou shalt receive a mighty fist instead.
                    [*They run. The TIE fighters pursue them,*
                    firing and knocking down Rey and Finn.
                              Finn is briefly unconscious.
What ho! Say, thou hast fallen. Wake, O wake!   100
FINN   [*waking:*] Confusion, lady. Tell me: art thou well?
REY   O, man of laughable intentions: ay.
This time, take thou my hand, and I shall lead.
                              [*Rey lifts Finn to his feet*
                              and they run toward the shipyard.
FINN   Our feet cannot outrun their laser blasts!
REY   We'll not have need, for we shall make escape   105
In that quad jumper.
FINN   —Where a pilot find?
REY   Search nowhere but before thine eyes: 'tis I!
FINN   Thou? Wondrous lady! What of that ship yon?
REY   Nay, 'tis but garbage fit for scrap, not flight.
                    [*The TIE fighters shoot and destroy the quad*
                    jumper toward which Rey and Finn are running.
The garbage shall suffice. Pray, let us go!   110
                         [*They run toward the other ship,*
                         which is the Millennium Falcon.
BB-8   Fligroil zoozblee flig zzwaflit blavblox blee
Blavzoon blikbloo blisflit flib zoomrooq blee!

REY   The gun position's there, below the decks—
                   I prithee, hie thee there and make defense.
                         [Finn moves downstage to the gunner position.

FINN   *[yelling:]* Hast thou e'er flown this vessel vast and

                                              old? 115

REY   It hath known naught of flight these many years.

FINN   The guns are here, yet they shake to and fro.
                   I can do this, and shall—I will not fail.
                        [Rey turns on the controls in the cockpit.

REY   I can do this, and shall—I will not fail.
                   Controls engag'd, we fly into the air—   120
                   O'er sandy dunes we soar above Jakku.
                   Until this moment life hath simple been:
                   Led only by mine instinct to survive,
                   Depending on no person but myself.
                   Belike Fate hath for me some other plan—   125
                   E'en with th'Resistance shall my path be join'd,
                   Knit closely unto them as skin to bone?
                   I take delight, such future to envision,
                   Ne'er hath my days such keen adventure known.
                   Tut, tut, it shall not be, nor may not, nay—   130
                   Out there, beyond the stars, my destiny
                   Shall not be found, for here I'm bound to wait.
                   Keen is my heart to see my family,
                   Yet when shall they return? Until that day,
                   Whene'er some undertaking doth arise   135
                   As has, today, come knocking on my door,
                   Lo, though the venture calls unto my heart—
                   Knocks deep within my soul to answer it—
                   E'en then, I know it may not, shall not, be.
                   Restricted is my life unto Jakku,   140

So may I see my family again
Once they have made their certain homecoming.
Meanwhile, I shall this bulky ship direct
If in the doing I may keep us safe.
Link'd are this droid and this man unto me—   145
Deliv'rance or disaster, come apace!

Enter UNKAR PLUTT *above, on balcony,*
witnessing the flight of the Millennium Falcon.

UNKAR   Yet what is this? That's mine! 'Tis mine, forsooth!
If ye shall steal from me, you'll know my steel!
                              [*Exit Unkar.*

FINN   [*to Rey:*] Stay low, and we may soon surpass our foes—
We shall confuse their tracking even thus.   150

REY   Small BB-8, I bid thee—hold thou tight!
I shall go 'round and lose these enemies.

BB-8   Flib flli flewzilf blox zzwaflig roilbluu roil!

FINN   These fighters do not miss the mark—we're hit.
Not fatally, yet more I'd not endure.   155

REY   With what art thou engag'd below the deck?
Shalt thou fire back, or let us be destroy'd?
Pray, take the gun and deftly strike withal!

FINN   I shall, and soon. Yet are the shields at full?

REY   Without copilot 'tis most difficult,   160
Yet I shall make it so.

FINN   [*aside:*]   —Try this foul gun—
'Tis hardly fit for operation, ha!
Now am I set—I fire to set us free!
                              [*Finn fires at the TIE fighters.*
Fie—we need cover quickly, else we die.

REY   We shall soon have some, if my ploy succeeds. 165
        I'll fly direct into the junkyards, there
        To keep us safe by th'armor of the ships
        That once did fall, so that we still may fly.
             [Rey pilots the Millennium Falcon
          into the wreckage of the junkyards of Jakku.
           Finn shoots and destroys a TIE fighter.
FINN   A-ha, thou fiend! My shot hath hit the mark.
REY   Well done, O comrade brave! Repeat it now. 170
FINN   *[aside:]* My skill increaseth with my fervor, yea.
        But what is this? My gun itself is struck,
        And hath turn'd lame. O, fie, what shall I do?
        [To Rey:] The cannon hath been stuck in forward aim—
        It shall not move, thus thou must dodge our foes. 175
REY   I'll bolder steps endeavor. Be prepar'd!
FINN   Prepar'd: so shall I be. And yet, for what?
             [Rey pilots the Millennium Falcon
               inside a crashed ship.
        Forbear! Shall we attempt this lunacy?
        For certain thou art wild—but not insane!
REY   Yet they would be the madder to give chase. 180
        Now out again, into the sunlit day,
        Where I shall play a classic pilot's ruse:
        To disengage the thrusters all, an 'twere
        The ship had broken down by some malfunction.
        It shall appear that we are bound to fall, 185
        As gravity doth work upon the ship
        And we do plummet swiftly to the ground.
        Then, in a trice, the thrusters reengage,
        And we make our escape. So, let it be!
             [Rey disengages the thrusters and

            lets the ship fall.

FINN   The final ship hath come within my sights: 190
       I shoot! By fortune carried to new heights!
           [Finn shoots and destroys
           the final TIE fighter. Exeunt.

SCENE 3.

Aboard the Finalizer.

Enter KYLO REN *and* LIEUTENANT MITAKA *on balcony.*

MITAKA   With deep regret, I must inform you, sir:
       We were unable to acquire the droid
       Who was but recently upon Jakku.
       It did escape our capture, fixèd fast
       Upon a stolen ship, which dock'd nearby: 5
       An old Corelli'n YT model freighter.
KYLO   Thou dost report the droid a freighter stole?
MITAKA   'Tis not precisely it; the droid had help.
       No confirmation hath yet been receiv'd, 10
       Yet we believe FN-2187
       Did aid the droid as it did make escape.
          [Kylo Ren brandishes his lightsaber,
          slashing the controls nearby.
KYLO   Incompetence beyond imagining!
       O, fie, that I this madness must endure—
       A fico for thine errant, bumbling face!
       The great First Order bested is by droids, 15
       Who ally 'gainst us with our own stormtroopers?
       Is this the folly-fallen end to which

The galaxy doth run with lout-like haste?
Ay, out upon it! Tilly-vally! Tush!
Hast thou aught more to say, lieutenant?

MITAKA   —Yea,   20
Although I fear the message mightily:
The two were by a girl accompanied—
                    [Kylo Ren uses the Force to pull
                    Mitaka toward him and grasps his neck.

KYLO   What girl? What is this nonsense here decreed?
                                        [Exeunt.

SCENE 4.

Aboard the Millennium Falcon.

Enter REY *and* BB-8.

REY   We shall depart, e'en briefly, from Jakku:
           So may the cruel First Order lose our trail.
BB-8   Zooz flitbluu flliblox blisflew zilfrooh flli
           Bluuzoon flig fllizoom blisblay roohflit zood.

Enter FINN.

REY   Thou wert amazing—
FINN   —Thou fantastic art   5
           At piloting, forsooth—
REY   —Thine aim was true.
FINN   O, take my humble thanks for thy kind words.
REY   Thou hast my gratitude for thine as well.
FINN   Where didst thou learn to fly with aptitude?
REY   I do not know—to speak the truth, the last   10
           Endeavor was quite foolish. But thy shooting—
           How well the final foe thou didst outdo!
FINN   Thy piloting did frame the perfect shot!
BB-8   Blox blayflib bloorooq bluuzooz zoonblip flig
           Flir roilblix blooblic blavzood blee, flig flib 15
           Blik bluublis flit blooflew reej roohblis zzwa
           Zoonflit blavbloo zood zilfroil zoom blooblee?
REY   Sweet BB-8, all shall be well, for he
           Is with the brave Resistance, as thou art.
           He shall take thee unto thy home at last.   20

We both will, ay—I shall, at least, go thither.
[*To Finn:*] Though we, by fate, have been together
                                 thrown,
Still I know not thy name.

FINN   —I am call'd Finn,
And at thy service firmly do I stand.
I prithee, fair one, what is thy name?

REY   —Rey,   25
The Rey who thanks thee for a bold escape.
             [*A pipe in the* Millennium Falcon *bursts
                 suddenly, sending smoke into the air.*
Alack! Give me thy swift assistance, Finn.

FINN   What is't? Shall our escape swift be withdrawn?
                  [*Rey climbs into a maintenance
                    bay to fix the ship.*

REY   The motivator hath been damagèd.
Pray find a Harris wrench and give it me.   30

FINN   How awful is the damage? Canst thou fix't?

REY   'Tis bad enow, if living is our wish.

FINN   Yet the First Order hunts for us e'en now—
We must this wretched system flee anon.

REY   Good BB-8 hath said th'Resistance base   35
Is hidden: knowledge thereof given on
A need-to-know foundation. Finn, if I
Am to transport you thither, I must know.

FINN   Is this the instrument that fits thy need?
            [*Finn throws the wrench to Rey, who disappears
              momentarily inside the bay. Finn beckons BB-8.*
Thou must unveil the secret of thy base   40
And its location unto me, my friend.

BB-8   Zooz zoonblip blooflit flewblis zzwa bleeblay!

FINN   I speak not all thy flits and blips and blays!
              Between we two, I am not from th'Resistance.
              To flee from the First Order is my need: 45
              Yet if thou shalt make known to us the base,
              I swear I'll bring thee thither. Ay, 'tis fair?
REY   [*emerging:*] A pilot's driver next. Say, where's thy base?
FINN   Fulfill thy mission: tell her, BB-8.
                        [*BB-8 looks back and forth between Rey and
                                        Finn in confusion.*
              [*Aside to BB-8:*] O, droid, I bid thee, search and thou
                                              shalt find   50
              Within my heart no rank, defiling trace.
BB-8   Zoom flliblox zoonflit flliflig roilblav blee
              Bluublee blikzoon flit flliblay bluu roilzoom.
REY   A-ha, the system of Ileenium!
FINN   The system of Ileenium, forsooth.   55
              Of course 'tis there, as I already knew.
              We must fly thither fast as fast can fly.
                              [*Finn hands Rey the pilot's driver.
                              He salutes BB-8, who salutes in
                              return using his droidly implements.*
REY   I'll drop ye at Ponemah Terminal.
              The bonding tape I do need next. 'Tis there.
FINN   Yet what of thee? Now, whither shalt thou go?   60
REY   I must with all due haste back to Jakku.
FINN   Wherefore must ev'ryone back to Jakku?
              What benefits do others find thereon?
              Though I would fain forget the horrid place,
              All others would with fervent haste return!   65
REY   The bonding tape is not that one. See it?
                              [*Finn searches but is unable to find it.*

Nay, nay, that one. The one to which I point.
Nay, nay, nay, nay! If we patch not the ship,
The large propulsion tank shall overflow
And flood the ship with gas most poisonous!   70
                   [BB-8 points his head to the part Rey needs,
                         which Finn picks up and hands to her.

FINN   Is't found?
REY   —Indeed, with little thanks to thee.
FINN   Yet thou thyself art pilot, wondrous skill'd.
          Thou canst fly anywhere. Thus: wherefore back?
          Need'st thou thy family, or paramour,
          A paramour most fine, with golden locks?   75
REY   The wherefore, verily, concerns thee not.
                   [The lights dim as a loud sound is heard.
                         The Millennium Falcon *is pulled*
                                inside a larger ship.
FINN   That sound portends some wicked twist of fate.
REY   Methinks thou hast it right; this bodes some ill.
                                [They run to the cockpit.
          Some other ship hath lock'd unto us tight—
          All our controls have been o'erridden quite.   80
FINN   I shall ascend, these new foes to behold.
                   [Finn climbs onto the controls, trying to see the
                         other ship and stepping on Rey in the process.
REY   Yet as thou dost, step not upon my pate!
          Canst see? What fight through yonder window breaks?
FINN   A ship o'ertakes us and consumes us full—
          It is the vile First Order, I am certain.   85
REY   What shall we do? Perchance there's aught will help.
FINN   Thou talk'dst a moment past of foulest gas,
          Fuel'd by some poison, eh?

REY   —I fix'd it well.

FINN   Canst thou unfix it, so to save our lives?
                    [*Rey, Finn, and BB-8 return to the maintenance*
                                        bay and climb inside.

REY   Come, BB-8, into the cargo bay.   90

FINN   I'll lift him down herein—alas, I fall—
              By George, the droid hath greater heft than I!

REY   Think'st thou this on the stormtroopers shall work?

FINN   Indeed—their masks can filter any smoke,
              But cannot filter toxins. They shall fall.   95

REY   [*aside:*] His knowledge of these troopers is immense—
              Th'Resistance brave is educated in
              The smallest details of their enemies.

                    They hide. Enter CHORUS.

CHORUS   Behold, now enter two familiar chaps,
              Their countenances older and grown wise: 100
              Though thirty years did o'er their lives elapse,
              Most happ'ly shall they come before your eyes.
                                        [*Exit Chorus.*

                    Enter HAN SOLO *and* CHEWBACCA.

HAN   O, vision I had never thought to see,
              O, sight beyond belief, an 'twere a dream,
              O, scene wherein I never thought to play,   105
              O, spectacle that warms a smuggler's heart—
              My ship, my strength, my soul, my ev'rything:
              Chewbacca, we are home.

CHEWBAC.   —Egh, egh, egh, auugh!¹
                  [Han and Chewbacca hear a noise. Han lifts the
                            hatch to expose Rey, Finn, and BB-8.

HAN   Where are the others? Where is all thy crew?
           And where the pilot who hath flown this ship?   110
REY   'Tis I: I am the pilot.
HAN   —Thou?
CHEWBAC.   —Egh, auugh!²
REY   My words are true: we only are aboard.
FINN   Thou canst that furry monster understand?
HAN   That furry monster understands thee, too,
           So prithee hold thy tongue, or be beshrew'd.   115
           Come up, out of the hold, and tell me quick:

---

¹ *Editor's translation:* O, thank the day, the great *Millenn'um Falcon*!
² *Editor's translation:* Nay, nay—since when were pilots made so young?

	Where didst thou find this ship? How came it thee?
REY	On Niima Outpost.
HAN	—On Jakku? That junkyard?
FINN	My thanks, good fellow. [*Aside, to Rey:*] 'Tis a junkyard, see?
HAN	[*to Chewbacca:*] I said we should the Western Reaches check. 120
CHEWBAC.	Egh![3]
HAN	—Who did own the ship? Was it Ducain?
REY	I took the ship from Unkar Plutt, who stole It from the Irving boys—as strong as oak And conifer—who hath, in turn, ta'en it From thy Ducain.
HAN	—Who stole the ship from me. 125 I prithee, when thou speak'st to him again, Tell bold Ducain Han Solo hath ta'en back The great *Millenn'um Falcon* once more—ha!— And ne'er shall from it separated be.
REY	This is the fam'd *Millenn'um Falcon*, what? 130 Thou art Han Solo?
HAN	—Yea, or us'd to be.
FINN	Han Solo, former gen'ral of th'Rebellion?
REY	Nay, he the smuggler of so many tales.
FINN	'Twas he, the fabl'd warring hero?
CHEWBAC.	—Auugh.[4]
REY	This is the ship that made the Kessel Run 135 In fourteen parsecs.

[3] *Editor's translation:* If I recall, 'twas I who did say so.
[4] *Editor's translation:* Belike 'tis he, yet speak in softer tones: In truth, my dear friend's head is large enow.

HAN   —Twelve! [*Aside:*] Fourteen, O pish!
O, ship, belovèd ship, how miss'd I thee.
[*To Rey and Finn:*] Yet wait, what is this oversight I spy?
Some idle-headed moof-milker did place
An ill compressor on th'ignition line!   140

REY   'Twas Unkar Plutt. Methought it was a blunder;
It doth too much o'erstrain—

HAN   —The hyperdrive.
[*Aside:*] Who is this lass, whose knowledge doth
     surprise?
It seems she hath both fortitude and skill,
A pilot unto whom I'd give respect   145
Were she not young enow to be my daughter,
Or—were I honest—mayhap granddaughter.
How sad the day when hath a Solo turn'd
Unto a song sung in a childish treble,
With pipes and whistles in his sound. Alas,   150
While years have pass'd I have, methinks, grown old.
Still, I am not so elderly that I
Have lost my tricks: I'll put them to the test
And test their mettle with a challenge new.
[*To Chewbacca:*] I prithee, Chewie, place them in a
     pod 155
And drop them on the nearest planet.

CHEWBAC.   —Auugh![5]

REY   Nay, cast us not aside so brazenly.
We need thy help.

HAN   —My help?

REY   —This little droid

---

[5] *Editor's translation:* As thou dost say, 'twill be most surely done.

	Must unto the Resistance fly anon!	
FINN	He hath obtain'd a map with which we'll find	160
	Luke Skywalker—a-ha! Thy face is plain:	
	The name I speak familiar is to thee.	
	Thou art the selfsame Solo who fought once	
	With the Rebellion 'gainst the former Empire.	
	Thy canst not feign that look: thou knewest him.	165
HAN	Indeed, I knew Luke well; a brother was	
	He unto me. [*A sound is heard.*] Fie, say no rathtar hath	
	Escap'd its bonds and runneth fast and free.	

> [*Han Solo runs from the* Millennium Falcon
> *with the others in pursuit.*

FINN	What's this? Speak'st thou of filthy rathtars now?	
	Thou haul'st no rathtars on this freighter, true?	170
HAN	I do haul rathtars on this freighter true.	
	Yet this next situation may prove worse:	
	The Guavian Death Gang hath boarded us—	
	Perforce they track'd us hither from Nantoon.	
REY	What is a rathtar?	
HAN	—Large and dangerous.	175
FINN	Know'st thou of th'Massacre of Trillia?	
REY	Nay, naught.	
FINN	—Such is unto thy benefit.	
HAN	I captur'd three of them as we unto	
	King Prana flew. They are within the holds.	
FINN	Three rathtars? How? They are nefarious!	180
	I fain would have thee tell me how 'twas done.	
HAN	Once I did travel with a larger crew.	
FINN	[*aside:*] O, dreadful notion, this!	

CHEWBAC.	—Egh, auugh, auugh, egh![6]
BB-8	Zooz zzwablis roilzoon zzwablox blicrooq blik!

                       [Han opens a hatch in the floor.

HAN	Pray, crawl inside and stay until I say.	185
	Think not, e'en for an instant, of once more	
	Appropriating the *Millenn'um Falcon*.	
REY	Agreed. What of the droid, small BB-8?	
HAN	With me shall he remain, until the gang	
	Hath gone. You three may then go on your way.	190
FINN	Where are the rathtars hidden? What of them?	

                   [A large rathtar tongue appears, striking the
                                window near Finn.

HAN	Thou hast found one. Congratulations, sirrah.	
REY	What shalt thou do?	
HAN	—What e'er hath been my wont:	
	Employ my tongue to rescue me.	

                   [Rey and Finn hide beyond the hatch.

CHEWBAC.	—Egh, auugh![7]	
HAN	Thy charge is baseless! It hath work'd each time.	195

Enter BALA-TIK *and other members of the* GUAVIAN DEATH GANG.

BALA-TIK	Han Solo, thou smuggler, scoundrel, rogue,
	thou art a dead man walking.
HAN	What ho, good Bala-Tik? What aileth thee?

---

[6] *Editor's translation:* Your rathtar is the emperor for diet:
  We fat all creatures else to fat ourselves;
  The crew did fat themselves for rathtars' meals.

[7] *Editor's translation:* A jest, forsooth! When hath thy tongue e'er solv'd
  A problem sans creating seven more?
  It ne'er hath work'd, in all our years together.

BALA-TIK   The problem is thee and thy lack of wit. We did give thee
             fifty thousand for the task thou hast not done.   200
REY   [*aside to Finn:*] Canst see them?
FINN   [*aside to Rey:*]   —Nay, they are too far aside.
BALA-TIK   Thou likewise hast ta'en fifty thousand from Kanjiklub.
             Ne'er hath a man made so many foes as thee.
HAN   Pray tell me thou hast not plac'd trust in them,
             Those base, ill-temper'd, short-of-stature knaves.   205
             How long have we been colleagues, Bala-Tik?
REY   [*aside to Finn:*] They carry blasters.
FINN   [*aside to Rey:*]   —Yea, full many, too.
BALA-TIK   Ask not how long we have known one another.
             Ask rather how much longer our acquaintance
             shall be. The answer, methinks, is not long. Thou   210
             art not long for life, unless thou canst make repayment.
HAN   Thou thinkest hunting rathtars costs but little?
             The money thou didst give me I have spent.
BALA-TIK   'Tis not we alone, for Kanjiklub also desires their
             investment return'd anon.   215
HAN   I ne'er did make a deal with Kanjiklub.
BALA-TIK   Those words speak thou to Kanjiklub, not me.

             Enter TASU LEECH *and other members of* KANJIKLUB.

HAN   O, Tasu Leech, join our festivities.
             'Tis fine to see thee here—thy men as well.
TASU   Yongari, Solo. Si digida manaria. Yowegah, Solo.   220
HAN   O, gentles, tell me, wherefore do you fret?
             You shall have what was promis'd, I shall swear't.
             Hath e'er Han Solo fail'd delivery?
BALA-TIK   Aye.

TASU	Sigi ginna manayea, beh.	225
HAN	'Tis twice, thou say'st? What was the second time?	
BALA-TIK	Thy game is old, as thou art. No soul remaineth in the galaxy for thee to swindle, cheat, and betray.	
TASU	Fennemana see na!	
BALA-TIK	Another sight doth interest me as well—that BB unit a'rolling 'round thy heels. The First Order searcheth e'en now for one such as this. Two errant fugitives, as well.	230
HAN	Thy words do fall like summer rain upon Mine ears, for they are unanticipated. No news have I of fugitives or droids.	235
TASU	Kadio kanyo.	
REY	[aside to Finn:] Behold, the panel that controls the doors. If I, perchance, the circuits can o'erwrite, The blast doors shall be clos'd and trap the gangs.	
FINN	[aside to Rey:] The outside blast doors thou canst close from here?	240
REY	[aside to Finn:] If I reset the fuses, it shall be.	

            [Rey presses a button on the control panel.
                      The doors do not close,
               but a growling sound is heard.

HAN	I have a feeling bad about this sound.	
REY	[aside to Finn:] Alas!	
FINN	[aside to Rey:] —Now wherefore sayest thou "alas"?	
REY	[aside to Finn:] Those fuses I did switch ought not be switch'd.	
BALA-TIK	Kill the smuggler and the Wookiee, and bring the droid to me!	245

Enter RATHTARS 1, 2, *and* 3, *devouring members*
of the GUAVIAN DEATH GANG *and* KANJIKLUB.

RATHTAR 1	[*sings:*] 'Tis now the time to eat, to eat!
RATHTAR 2	[*sings:*] A hearty meal, a treat, a treat!
RATHTAR 3	[*sings:*] My stomach they'll complete, complete!
RATHTAR 2	[*sings:*] This human feast I greet, I greet!

   250

[Exeunt Han, Chewbacca, and BB-8,
fleeing from the rathtars. Rey and Finn emerge
from hiding severally.

FINN	This was a grand mistake, and maybe fatal!
REY	Mayhap the largest I have ever made.
	Pray, let us hence—away from these sharp sounds!
	How do these beasts appear? What is their form?

[Rey and Finn turn a corner and see a rathtar.

| FINN | 'Tis that. That is their raging, putrid form. |

   255

| RATHTAR 3 | [*sings:*] Two more of them we chase, we chase! |
| RATHTAR 1 | [*sings:*] Our table they shall grace, shall grace! |

RATHTAR 2   [*sings:*] Although from us they race, they race!
RATHTAR 1   [*sings:*] We'll follow them apace, apace!
FINN   Pray, follow near, go hence!
REY   —Art thou most sure?   260
                    [A rathtar's tentacle catches Finn's leg.
RATHTAR 3   [*sings:*] I have him by the leg, the leg!
RATHTAR 1   [*sings:*] Anon for life he'll beg, he'll beg!
RATHTAR 2   [*sings:*] We'll hang him on a peg, a peg!
RATHTAR 3   [*sings:*] And munch him like an egg, an egg!
                    [Exeunt rathtars, dragging Finn with them.
REY   Alas, my Finn! So quickly met and lost—   265
              I'll save thee yet, though it be Rey's last act!
                         [Rey notices the control panel.
              The panel of controls—this shall suffice.
              If I am careful (yea, unlike before),
              I may succeed in shutting all the doors
              Between the rathtars and my loyal Finn.   270
              Now carefully, most carefully: and to it!

              REY *presses a button on the control panel.*
              A RATHTAR *shrieks offstage. Enter* FINN.

FINN   The rathtar held me fast within its grip,
              And certain was 'twould be my final breath,
              Yet then the door by happenstance fast clos'd,
              And finally—
REY   [*aside:*]   —He wonders at my deed,   275
              Whereof he knoweth naught. Yet we've no time
              For wondering. [*To Finn:*] 'Twas fortunate indeed.
              More of thy tale I'd hear another time,
              Yet now let's fly ere other rathtars come.

Enter HAN SOLO, CHEWBACCA, *and* BB-8 *pursued
by a member of the* GUAVIAN DEATH GANG.

HAN   We must unto the ship, or eaten be.   280
             These doors, however, must first be unlock'd
             Before we can th'*Millenn'um Falcon* reach.
             Pray give me thy protection, Chewie.
                        [*A member of the Guavian Death Gang
                             shoots Chewbacca in the shoulder.*

CHEWBAC.   —Auugh![8]
                        [*Han takes Chewbacca's gun and shoots the foe.*

HAN   [*aside:*] This mighty blaster crossbow hath a kick—
             Thus shall I shoot the door and set us free!   285
             Now come withal, for we shall fly anon!

REY   Han—

HAN   —Thou must close the door behind us now.
             [*To Finn:*] And thou shalt help Chewbacca to the ship.
                        [*They rush into the* Millennium Falcon.
                        Han begins preparing the cockpit and Rey takes
                                             the copilot's seat.*

             What inappropriate presumption's this?
             What art thou doing?

REY   —Unkar Plutt install'd   290
             A fuel pump in the ship. If 'tis not prim'd,
             We shall be bound for nowhere.

HAN   —Fie on him!

REY   Also, unless I am inaccurate,
             Thou art, it seemeth, one co-pilot short.

HAN   I have one there, beyond the cockpit, hurt.   295

_____

[8] *Editor's translation:* Alack, the fire hath burn'd my Wookiee bones!

	Watch thou the thrust; at lightspeed we'll depart.
REY	From here, within the bay? Is't possible?
	We'll either 'scape the hangar or be hung!
HAN	Ne'er do I question possibility
	Until the deed already hath been done. 300

Enter RATHTAR 3.

RATHTAR 3	[*sings:*] O, ye five shall not flee, not flee,
	Until you are in me, in me!
HAN	When I awoke upon this pleasant morn,
	This was not how methought the day would go.
	Now angle up the shields, and we fly! 305
FINN	No bother 'tis, we fully are prepar'd.

> [*Finn looks for materials to bind Chewbacca's*
> *arm and pulls a remote control out of a bag.*

	[*Aside:*] For what use was this ancient-looking tool?
	Some sphere made for a sporting pleasure game?
	My questions shall not find their answer here,
	And other matters are more pressing, Finn. 310
HAN	O, fail me not, my long-belovèd ship!
	Yet wherefore doth the vessel not respond?
REY	'Tis the compressor.
HAN	[*aside:*] —Ay, again she's right.

> [*The* Millennium Falcon *bursts*
> *into hyperspace. Rathtar 3 flies off.*

Enter BALA-TIK *on balcony.*

BALA-TIK	[*into communicator:*] Inform the dread
	First Order that the droid they so desire 315

is in the clutches of Han Solo,
the smuggler and knave, aboard the *Millennium*
Falcon.

HAN   We fly, bound for the galaxy's safe border—
Mayhap this shall restore my life to order.

[*Exeunt.*

SCENE 5.

Inside Starkiller Base.

Enter SUPREME LEADER SNOKE, KYLO REN, *and* GENERAL HUX.

SNOKE   The droid shall soon unto the pitiful
Resistance be deliver'd. This, in turn,
Shall lead them thither, unto Skywalker:
He, last of all the Jedi. If he's found,
A race of bold new Jedi may arise.   5

HUX   O, Supreme Leader, 'tis for me to bear
The grave responsibility—

SNOKE   —Tut, tut!
Our strategy, my general, must change.

HUX   The weapon is prepar'd and ready stands:
Methinks the time hath come to see it us'd.   10
We shall destroy the government that doth
Give its support unto the vile Resistance:
E'en the Republic. Sans their friends to bring
Protection, the Resistance shall be weak
And vulnerable, too. They shall be stopp'd   15
Ere they can reach Skywalker where he hides.

SNOKE   Get hence and guide the preparations now.

HUX	Indeed, my lord, with joy it shall be done.

[Exit Hux.

SNOKE   Hark! There hath been a swift awakening—
         Canst feel it?

KYLO   —Yea.

SNOKE   —For thee there's something more.   20
         The droid we seek is on th'*Millenn'um Falcon,*
         Withal thy father: e'en Han Solo, he.

KYLO   The man doth nothing mean—and less—to me.

SNOKE   E'en thou, the master of the Knights of Ren,
         Hath ne'er such challenge fac'd as lies herein.   25

KYLO   Your training is sufficient unto me,
         And, therefore, I shall not seducèd be.

SNOKE   Ahh, we shall see. Indeed, we two shall see.

[Exit Snoke.

KYLO   My father? O, a complication dire—
         The father who did help to give me life,   30
         The father who did raise me to know good,
         The father who did nourish all my skills,
         The father whom I did, at last, reject.
         Reenters he unto my life e'en now?
         Yet worse: the partner of mine enemies,   35
         The keeper of that which I would obtain,
         A barrier unto my long'd-for aim.
         I am no longer kin to Solo, nay:
         My family is here, within this base,
         The good First Order and the Knights of Ren.   40
         No other family do I desire—
         Especially no smuggler, base and crude,
         And ignorant of how to use the Force.
         Although my feelings do betray me still,

I must be strong, remember my dark call,   45
And shun the folly pulling me toward him.
No son of Solo I, no longer Ben—
From now, I am entirely Kylo Ren.

                                       [Exit.

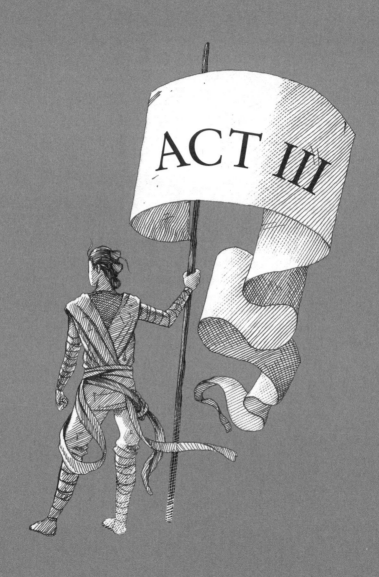

SCENE 1.

Aboard the Millennium Falcon, *on the planet Takodana,*
and inside Starkiller Base.

Enter HAN SOLO *and* REY, *in the cockpit*
of the Millennium Falcon. *Enter* FINN *with* CHEWBACCA
severally, mending the Wookiee's shoulder.

HAN	Too many years of too infrequent use
	Hath left the swift *Millenn'um Falcon* tir'd
	And prone to small malfunction, disrepair.
	Just now, a new electrical o'erload.
REY	Methinks I'll solve the riddle in a trice. 5
HAN	The coolant leaketh, too.
REY	—If thou transfer'st
	The pow'r auxiliary unto the—
HAN	The secondary tank! A-ha, I see.
	[*Aside:*] Again, we think as two halves of a whole.
CHEWBAC.	Egh, auugh![9]
FINN	—If thou'dst not wiggle to and fro, 10
	Belike I now could proffer thee some aid.
	Forget thou not that I am here to help.
	O, cannot someone tame this hairy fiend?

Enter BB-8.

BB-8	Flit flliblik blicrooq blooflir zoomblav blee!

---

[9] *Editor's translation:* Who taught thee how to mend an arm—a rancor?

CHEWBAC.   Auugh! Auugh![10]

BB-8   —Bluu zzwablox roil flib zzwa
                                                 flewblis!   15
                                         [Exit BB-8, in fear.

HAN   *[to Finn:]* If thou dost hurt Chewbacca, thou shalt know
             The menace of Han Solo's fearsome ire!

FINN   Hurt him? O, fine assessment of the scene!
             He hath near kill'd me some six times thus far.
                              [Chewbacca grabs Finn by the throat
                                         and pulls him close.
             'Tis fine, I have no quarrel with thee, sir!   20

HAN   If here the hyperdrive should overheat,
             Methinks there shall be scatter'd bits and scraps
             Of Solo strewn around the galaxy.
                         [Rey pulls a wire loose and the ship settles.
             [Aside:] Amazing, her innate abilities!
             [To Rey:] Say, how didst thou resolve our quandary?   25

REY   I bypass'd the compressor, by my troth.

HAN   A simple trick. *[Aside:]* Good as the best. *[To BB-8:]*
                                                 Hence, ball!
                         [Han walks past BB-8 as he exits the cockpit,
                                approaching Chewbacca and Finn.

REY   *[aside:]* I thought he might, this once, be satisfied—
             How strange it is how I do wish to please him,
             Yet in his presence I am like a child,   30
             And he a hero of proportion grand.

CHEWBAC.   *[to Han:]* Egh, egh.[11]

---

[10] *Editor's translation:* Depart, thou orange tin—else face my wrath!

[11] *Editor's translation:* Afeard I am mine age begins to show,
    I was not fast enow in this last scuffle—
    This Wookiee's body moveth far too slow.

HAN   —Nay, speak not so. Thou didst
                                                            thy best,
            Which is, dear friend, all we can ask in life.
            Pray, put thy spirit and thy bones at ease.
            [*To Finn:*] Thou too, my lad, comportedst thyself well. 35
            Thou hast my thanks.

FINN   —Forsooth, my welcome's thine.
                                    [*Finn accidentally turns on a*
                                    nearby holochess game. Chewbacca
                                    looks on happily. Rey joins them.
            [*Aside:*] Behold, the rapture on the Wookiee's face!
            I'll warrant 'tis a fav'rite game of his.

HAN   Ye two are fugitives, saith Bala-Tik?

REY   The cruel First Order longeth for the map.   40
            Finn here is with the strong Resistance, though—
                                    [*Finn looks at Han guiltily.*
            Whilst I am but a petty scavenger.

HAN   Shall we see th'information they do seek,
            Which this small droid doth somehow now possess?

BB-8   Flew zoombloo zzwablic blayflir flli?

REY   —Indeed.   45
                        [*BB-8 projects the portion of the map he holds.*

HAN   The map is incomplete, a piece is gone.
            Since Luke did disappear have many search'd
            To bring him back, but all to no avail.

REY   Yet wherefore did he leave initially?

HAN   He tried to train a class of Jedi, yea,   50
            The next, new generation who would lead.
            One boy, however, his apprentice, hath
            Turn'd 'gainst Luke and destroy'd the plan entire.
            Luke felt responsible and went away.

FINN	Know'st thou what follow'd? Whither he did go? 55
HAN	There was but room for rumors, with no root.
	Full many tales and fables were conceiv'd.
	Those who did know him best bethought he went
	A'searching for the bygone Jedi temple.
REY	The Jedi, then, were real, as some do say. 60
HAN	Thus did I wonder once, when I was young,
	Methought 'twas all but hurly-burly talk—
	A power magical 'twixt light and dark—
	And yet, though it but seemeth mad: 'tis true.
	It is—in ev'ry particle, each bit, 65
	The smallest word or whisper of the Force,
	The briefest tale about the Jedi told,
	Each story that expands our universe,
	Each tiniest detail of reck'ning—true,
	And more fool we who do believe it not. 70

[*A sensor beeps.*
BB-8 extinguishes the projection.

CHEWBAC.	Egh, auugh![12]
HAN	—Nay, Chewie, thou shouldst rest
	thyself.
	[*To Rey and Finn:*] If you desire my help, then you shall
	ha't.
	We shall stop off and visit an old friend.
	The droid she shall deliver to its place,
	Whereby it may th'Resistance show the map. 75
	We have at Takodana now arriv'd—
	I'll make arrangements for ye both thereon.

---

[12] *Editor's translation:* I should attend unto the *Falcon*'s call.

          [They enter the cockpit as the
          ship emerges from lightspeed,
          headed for the surface of Takodana.

REY   My stars! Not in the galaxy entire
          Would I have thought existed so much green.

HAN   [*aside:*] 'Tis she is green, and wholly innocent,
          An 'twere a newborn babe were in my care.   80
                [Chewbacca, Rey, and BB-8 disembark
                       from the Falcon.

FINN   Lo, Solo, I know not what we shall find—

HAN   Didst thou, in youthful boldness, call me "Solo"?

FINN   Apologies, fair Han, or Master Solo,
          Whatever appellation thou prefer'st.
          Thou shouldst be fully cognizant of this: 85
          Within th'Resistance I am known for bigness.
          No small flywheel within the vast machine,

	But fit for larger things: a warrior—	
	Forsooth, a status unimpeachable,	
	A reputation of most fine repute.	90
	I have, therefore, a mark upon my life.	
	Shall there, herein, be found conspirators?	
	First Order cronies who would work me woe?	
HAN	Attend me, Bigness, thou hast problems more:	
	The lady shall find out the truth of thee—	95
	Their sex e'er have, and do, and always shall.	

> [*Han hands Finn a blaster, disembarks,*
> *and joins Rey, who stands alone.*
> *He hands her a blaster as well.*

	This blaster thou mayst need in times to come.	
REY	Methinks I have the wit to handle all.	
HAN	Thus think I, too; 'tis why I make the gift.	
	I prithee, take it. [*She does.*] Tell me, canst thou aim?	100
	Know'st thou its movements and what gives it fire?	
REY	The trigger pull'd, the fire doth follow on.	
HAN	A simpleton mayhap would so reply,	
	Yet 'tis not quite so simple as thou say'st.	
	Thou hast, still, much to learn. Hast thou a name?	105
REY	'Tis Rey.	
HAN	—Rey, verily. I did bethink	
	Me to take on more crew: a second mate,	
	A person who may render good assistance,	
	Match step with step Chewbacca and myself,	
	And who appreciates the *Falcon*, too.	110
REY	Is't possible thou offer'st me employment?	
HAN	We would be less than kin, still less be kind.	
	It promiseth a journey hazardous,	
	Small wages, bitter times, long months of dark	

| | Complete, a constant danger, thy return | 115 |
| | Most doubtful, and no honor in success. | |

REY   Thou offer'st me employment!

HAN   —I bethought on't:
             No pledge was made: I cannot be forsworn.

REY   [*aside:*] O, how my soul doth long to take this leap,
             To plunge into the deep whate'er befall,   120
             Yet softly calls the voice of duty still
             And keeps me sadly tether'd to the ground.
             [*To Han:*] If thou wert offering, I'd honor'd be,
             Yet cannot take the offer: I must home.

HAN   Jakku?

REY   —Already have I been too long.   125

HAN   Thy swift reply confoundeth all my wits.
             [*To Chewbacca:*] Good Chewie, pray inspect the ship
                                                with care.
             [*To Rey:*] Unfortunate it is; the Wookiee likes thee.
                         [*They walk toward Maz Kanata's castle.*

FINN   Remind me, Solo, wherefore are we here?

HAN   To put your droid upon a ship that's clean.   130

REY   Clean?

HAN   —Think'st thou 'twas by fortune's hand that we
             The *Falcon* with such ease did find? Nay, nay.
             If we with our mere scanners found the ship,
             Thou canst be sure the swift First Order cometh.
             If ye would render BB-8 unto   135
             The brave Resistance, Maz Kanata is
             Your simplest, best—and mayhap only—hope.

FINN   Can she be trusted, eh? This friend of thine?

HAN   Be calm and tarry on, lad, for Maz o'er
             The public house that thou wilt see hath been   140

Proprietor for lo these thousand years.
That said, this Maz doth not please ev'ryone:
'Tis best if you two let me speak. I pray,
Whate'er ye do, gape not.

REY   —At what?

HAN   —At aught.

They enter the castle. Enter MAZ KANATA *and many aliens
including* BAZINE, GRUMMGAR, GA-97, CAPTAIN ITHANO,
and QUIGGOLD, *all seated severally. Enter* CHORUS.

CHORUS   Now mark ye well, good viewers, what you see,   145
             Such varied characters are on display!
             For never hath there been such company
             As there, in Maz's castle, comes each day.
             Strange creatures form to make a splendid scene—
             There, to the side, some play a game of chance,   150
             See bulky Grummgar and his girl Bazine:
             This is the house of Maz—let your eyes dance!
                                 [Exit Chorus.

MAZ   Han Solo!
                          *[All in the castle fall silent
                                and stare at Han.*

HAN   [*aside:*]   —This was not the hop'd-for entrance.
             [*To Maz:*] Holla, Maz!

MAZ   —Where hast put my paramour?

HAN   Chewbacca worketh on the *Falcon*, Maz.   155

MAZ   I've ta'en a liking to that Wookiee, ay.
             Thou must need something, else thou wouldst not come.
             Belike thy need is desperate, as well,
             So let us to it. Thither, sit with me.

[*Bazine, Grummgar, and GA-97*
notice BB-8 as he rolls by.

GA-97   [*into communicator:*] Transmit to the Resistance this
                                                    report: 160
             The droid for which they search hath hither come.
BAZINE   [*into communicator:*] Inform the dread First Order:
                                            their lost droid
             Is here on Takodana. Come, at once!

             All freeze. Enter KYLO REN *on balcony,*
             holding the mask of DARTH VADER.

KYLO   Forgive me, grandfather, again I feel't,
             The call to light, which Supreme Leader Snoke   165
             Doth sense. Unfold, before my sight, once more

The power of the dark side of the Force.
Then naught shall stand athwart my fervent plans.
Show me, I bid thee, so that I may end
What thou, in all thy wisdom, didst begin.   170

> [*Exit Kylo Ren. Han, Maz, Rey,*
> *and Finn sit around a table.*
> *BB-8 stands on the floor nearby.*

HAN   We seek safe passage for this little droid,
            Which carrieth a map to Luke Skywalker.

MAZ   A map that leads to Skywalker himself?
            Ha, ha! Thou findest thyself in the mire,
            Where ever it doth seem thou landest, Han.   175

HAN   Maz, canst thou get the droid to Leia?

MAZ   —Nay.
            Too long hast thou been fleeing from this fight.
            Han, nyagi neko toya—go thou home!

HAN	My Leia doth not wish to see my face.
FINN	We travel'd far, just to entreat thy help. 180
REY	This fight of which thou speak'st—what dost thou
	mean?
MAZ	The only fight that we need ever know:
	Against the dark side. Lo these many years
	I've seen the many forms that evil takes:
	The cruel, bloodthirsty Sith, the Empire rank, 185
	And now the vile First Order in their place.
	Like wolves who run in packs, with fur most black,
	Or like a shroud pull'd over the deceas'd,
	Or like the dark that comes in bleakest night,
	They spread their shadows o'er the galaxy. 190
	They must be fac'd and fought by each of us.
FINN	No fight 'gainst the First Order can be won.
	Look 'round this shady place: for surety
	Our faces have been recogniz'd by some.
	Belike the swift First Order draweth near, 195
	E'en as we speak in awe and fear of it.

> [Maz adjusts her spectacles and
> looks more closely at Finn. She climbs
> on the table to get closer to him.

	What is this folly? Solo, canst thou tell?
HAN	I know not, but I do not like its look—
	It seems she looks on thee with special eyes.
MAZ	When one lives long enow, one doth observe 200
	The selfsame eyes appearing in a host
	Of people. I have seen thine eyes before:
	The fearful eyes of one who wants to run,
	The craven eyes of one who fears a fight,
	The wounded eyes of one who hath seen evil, 205

	The doubtful eyes of one who longs for truth.
FINN	Thou know'st me not, nor that from which I come,
	What I experienc'd before this time.
	Thou canst not know the ways of the First Order
	As I do: they shall bring our swift defeat. 210
	Forsooth, we all should run, not I alone.

[Maz returns to her seat.

MAZ   Look yonder, see the two a'sitting there?
          They shall trade work for transportation to
          The Outer Rim, where thou canst disappear.

REY   Finn?

FINN   —Rey, pray follow thou along with me.   215

REY   But what of BB-8? Our task still calls—
          Thy base it is to which he must return.

BB-8   Flew roilzoon flliblic bleezooz blisblik blee
          Roohzoom flit bleerooq flirzilf flig blayblee.

FINN   I cannot—fear too much doth lead my course.   220

[Finn hands his blaster back to Han.

HAN   'Tis thine, lad—thou may yet have need of it.

[Finn moves to another table and sits
with Captain Ithano and Quiggold.
Rey follows him, and BB-8 follows her.

MAZ   [*to Han:*] Who is the girl, and whence comes she?
                                              Dost know?

[Exeunt Han and Maz in conversation.
Exeunt Bazine, Grummgar, GA-97, and other aliens.

QUIGGOLD [*to Finn:*] Dah igga ga.

ITHANO   —Ni ante ante, beh.

FINN   Good sirs, it rumor'd is that you fine folk
          Can take me swiftly to the Outer Rim.   225

REY   [*approaching:*] What art thou doing?

FINN   [*to Ithano and Quiggold:*]   —Pray, fly not sans me.
                                         [*Finn steps aside with Rey.*

REY   I bid thee, look around: thou canst not leave.
            I shall not let thee so abandon me.

FINN   Forsooth, I'm not the man thou think'st I am.

REY   What dost thou mean?

FINN   —Foh, I am not Resistance!   230
            No hero I upon a fearless task,
            No bold adventurer on fate-fill'd quest,
            No frank and gallant man with noble aim,
            No clever soldier, fast of wit and shrewd.
            I am—or was—a rank stormtrooper first.   235
            Like ev'ry trooper, I was taken from
            A family whom I shall never know
            And rais'd but for one thing alone: to kill.
            Then on Jakku, I my first battle fac'd
            And made a choice: I would not fight for them,   240
            Not slaughter, not destroy, not feed their hate.
            Then did I run and found thee at the end.
            Thou look'dst on me as no one had before.
            Fill'd was I with the shame of th'man I was,
            Yet ne'er shall I return, not even if   245
            I live forever. With the rank First Order
            I have progress'd from Finn to finishèd.
            Now, face-to-face, I beg, Rey: come with me.

REY   I beg thee in return, Finn: do not leave.

FINN   It cannot be; fear doth o'erwhelm desire.   250
            I prithee, Rey, take care of thy kind self.
                    [*Exeunt Finn, Captain Ithano, and Quiggold.*

REY   O, misery, abandon'd yet again—
            Resounding grief within my very core!

My lot, belike, is ne'er to know a bond
As strong as that Fate doth to others bring.   255
Yet set aside these thoughts—what is that noise?
Hear I some child who cries somewhere below.
Am I imagining? I shall descend,
Perchance to find the child and ease my mind.
Climb down these steps, with BB-8 behind.   260
Herein I see no child, yet hear the call.
It seems to come from deep within this chest,
Left here in this dark room—but can it be?
Do voices speak within insensate things?
Ope I the lid and see what is inside.   265
Feast, eyes—a lightsaber! Hold it I must!
Lo, strange and forceful visions do befall:
Electric lights within a chamber vast,
I fall as it beginneth to collapse!

A hooded man who reacheth to a droid—   270
Alas, behind me, people slain by foes,
Now, people dress'd in black, all menacing,
Dark emanates from one with wicked mask.
Here I, a child, beset by fear and want
E'en as the ones I love did fly away.   275
Releas'd from this, I hear a voice say "Rey."
How now, convey'd unto a forest scene,
A red lightsaber meant to do me harm!
Ne'er let this be, O, let this vision cease!

> REY *is released from her vision,*
> *stumbling to the floor. Enter* MAZ KANATA.

BB-8   Zoozflew blikrooh flig zzwablox flitrooq flib   280
        Zoom bleeblis zilfflir blee flitroil fligroil?
REY   What happen'd? I should not have gone therein.
        I dreamt a dream inside.
MAZ   —And so did I.
REY   Well, what was thine?
MAZ   —That dreamers often lie.
REY   Upon the ground while they do dream things true.   285
MAZ   O, then I see keen Maz hath been with you.
        She is the vision giver, and she comes
        In shape no bigger than an agate stone
        On the forefinger of a Jedi Knight.
        The lightsaber that thou didst touch was Luke's,   290
        And ere 'twas his, it was his father's, too—
        Now doth it call to thee, thy heart, thy soul.
REY   I must return unto Jakku anon.
MAZ   Han told me all. O, child, I see thine eyes—

| | Already thou dost know the truth entire: | 295 |

Already thou dost know the truth entire: 295
They on whom thou dost wait, there on Jakku,
Shall ne'er return. Yet someone else still may.

REY Thou meanest Luke.

MAZ   —The deep belonging thou
Dost seek is not behind thee, but before.
I am no Jedi, yet I know the Force.   300
It moveth through each thing and doth surround
Each one of us. Pray close thine eyes and feel't.
The light hath been there e'er—guide thee it shall.
The lightsaber—take it, and let it lead.

REY Nay, this is not the future I do seek,   305
Nor is't the course on which I set my steps.
That lightsaber I would not touch once more;
A part within this scene I look'd not for.

    [Exit Rey, running away. Exeunt Maz and BB-8.

SCENE 2.

At Starkiller Base.

Enter GENERAL HUX *addressing companies of* STORMTROOPERS.

HUX This is the weak Republic's final hour,
The end of those who foster such unrest.
They shall observe the strong First Order's pow'r!
E'en now, far hence, th'Republic false and dour
Doth lie unto a galaxy oppress'd.   5
This is the weak Republic's final hour!
Supporting the Resistance, they devour
All chance for peace, which else might manifest.

They shall observe the strong First Order's pow'r!
This fierce machine you built shall make them cow'r,   10
And bring an end unto the Senate pest—
This is the weak Republic's final hour!
Th'Republic's fleet, once a colossal tow'r,
Shall crumble like an old bird's feeble nest—
They shall observe the strong First Order's pow'r!   15
At our vast might and boldness all shall glow'r,
Then bow—our eminence at last confess'd.
This is the weak Republic's final hour—
They shall observe the strong First Order's pow'r!
                              [*All salute General Hux.*

TROOPER   All is prepar'd to bring destruction dire.   20
HUX   Then let it be! I bid thee, sirrah, fire!

Starkiller Base fires at a distant planetary system. Enter CHORUS.

CHORUS   I bid ye, look away or be undone,
            As this Starkiller weapon takes its aim.
            For with the vim and vigor of a sun,
            Not one, but many planets doth it maim.   25
            Full millions, billions meet a sudden end,
            Bereft of hope, of love, of life, of all,
            Ne'er more to know the laughter of a friend,
            Ne'er more to hear a tender lover's call,
            Ne'er more to see the growing of a child,   30
            Ne'er more to sing life's joyful melody.
            This lunacy of the First Order wild
            Doth shake, at once, the whole sad galaxy.
                                        [*Exeunt.*

SCENE 3.

On the planet Takodana.

Enter HAN SOLO *and* CHEWBACCA, *looking to the skies.*
Enter FINN *severally, running to them.*

FINN   I near had left, had flown fore'er away,
Until I saw this fire light up the sky.
O, shocking day! The vile First Order hath
Fulfill'd its vengeance on the galaxy.
But soft, whilst we look heav'nward, where is Rey?   5
                    [Exeunt.

Enter REY, *aside.*

REY   Confus'd by visions I did not desire,
My heart hath turn'd to something less robust—
The blood all turn'd water—and in fear
I ran, and do run still, and e'er may run.

Enter BB-8, *pursuing* REY.

BB-8   Flig flewblay roohblik flliblis flitroil rooh   10
Zoomblee rooqflir flib zoonblip blooblix flew?
REY   Say, wherefore hast thou hither follow'd me?
Thou must return, the others fly withal.
BB-8   Flig zzwazoom rooh, bloxflew zilfrooh zooz blay?
REY   I must depart and fly back to Jakku.   15
Sweet BB-8, thou art far more important
Than know'st thou. Go, thy mission to fulfill.
       [A sound is heard in the sky. Rey looks up.

Alas, a sound of ships and there—above
The trees and drawing nearer—horrid ships
Mark the First Order's entrance on the scene.   20
                                        [*Exeunt.*

Enter HAN SOLO, CHEWBACCA, *and* FINN *led by* MAZ KANATA.
                She shows them the lightsaber.

MAZ   This Rey did see and run; I did acquire
             It many moons ago and kept it safe.
HAN   Luke's lightsaber! Where camest thou by it?
MAZ   A worthy question, ask'd another time,
             Yet now we cannot stop for myths and tales.   25
             Take it and find thy friend, I bid thee, Han.
                                [A blast rocks Maz's castle.
             The beasts—they come and shall not be deterr'd.
                                        [*Exeunt.*

                Enter REY *and* BB-8, *aside.*

REY   The battle is upon us, and I'll not
             Sit idly by—come blaster, gift of Han,
             And bring the fire that else they'd send on me!   30
             Alack, the wretched safety is engag'd—
             Han was, belike, correct to question me
             And my ability to fire the weapon.

             Enter two STORMTROOPERS, *firing at* REY.

             Feel ye my fire—Rey shall not die today!
                        [Rey fires at the stormtroopers, hitting one.

Enter a legion of STORMTROOPERS *severally.*
Enter KYLO REN *near them, descending from his shuttle.*

TROOPER   My liege, the droid was witness'd trav'ling west—   35
              His sole companion was a lowly girl.

KYLO   A girl—those words have prick'd mine ears before!
                          [Exit Kylo Ren, looking for Rey.

REY   *[to BB-8:]* Thou shalt press on and keep thyself well hid.
              I'll give thee cover—thou must make escape!

BB-8   Zooz flliblay roohblox bloo flewblip blav blee   40
              Blav fllibluu roil flirroil rooqblis zoomblee
              Blikblee reej flitzilf roohzood bleeblic blee
              Flib zzwazooz flig blayzzwa blox flliflew zoon.

REY   I hope so, too, kind BB-8. Now, go!
                      [Exeunt Rey and BB-8 severally.

Enter HAN SOLO, MAZ KANATA, CHEWBACCA,
and FINN, *emerging from the castle. Chaos reigns.*

HAN   The battle's on, as in the days of yore.   45
              Stormtroopers never were a welcome sight,
              And still I find them loathsome, by my troth.
              My skill withal a blaster in my hand
              Remaineth, though my body hath grown old.
              Behold how they like sitting marks do fall—   50
              Without e'en looking may I bring them down.
              I would not boast were I not so endow'd.
              Wish you to skirmish with Han Solo, eh?
              Prepare, therefore, to speak your final words.
              Come, Chewie, we must to the *Falcon* fly.   55

MAZ   *[to Finn:]* Keen Rey and BB-8—they need thee now.

        Go find them, quickly. Bring them back alive.

FINN   For certain—yet a weapon do I need.

MAZ   The lightsaber thou holdest in thy hand:

        Thou hast a weapon—use it faithfully.   60

             [Finn activates Luke's lightsaber. Exit Maz.

FINN   I feel the strength within this pulsing light,

        And Finn is now equipp'd to join the fight!

HAN   *[to Chewbacca:]* Can I try out thy crossbow blaster?

CHEWBAC.   —Egh.[13]

             [Han shoots Chewbacca's blaster.

HAN   A worthy weapon, powerful and true!

       Enter FN-2199, *a powerful stormtrooper,*

       holding a Z6 baton. He bears down on FINN.

FN-2199   Thou fobbing, hedge-born traitor, lout, and scum!   65

        We once were friends, and train'd together, aye—

        But now hast thou become a turncoat, drawn

        To the Resistance and its errant ways!

        Prepare to meet thy doom, for naught exists

        As low as he who hath betray'd his friends!   70

FINN   My past comes from the dead to haunt me here:

        Then have at thee, thou fiend, and feel my bite.

                    [They duel.

        O, mighty man, who e'er did bring me fear.

        I'll warrant I'm unequal in this fight.

             [FN-2199 nearly overtakes Finn when he is

              struck with a blaster shot. He falls, and Han

---

[13] *Editor's translation:* O, silly friend of mine who think'st the blast
   Is always keener on the other side.

                           and Chewbacca run to Finn.

HAN   Say, Bigness, art thou well?

FINN   —Full many thanks.   75
              Thou here didst render my life back to me.

TROOPER   [*approaching:*] Move not! Be still! Lo, TK-338,
              Our targets are in watchful custody.

HAN   We have been ta'en, our next steps thwarted, yea—
              Yet what is this commotion in the air?   80
              More ships approach, not the First Order, nay:
              It is the brave Resistance, come to save!

Enter a legion of RESISTANCE X-WING PILOTS, *including* POE DAMERON,
firing at the STORMTROOPERS. *Enter* BB-8 *severally.*

POE   This is a world of sweet and sours, and thus
              Let victory be sweet as we plunge straight
              Ahead into the fray! Let not their sour   85
              And savage dogs make ye afeard or cautious,
              My pilots true, for we shall win the day!

PILOTS   Aye!
                 [*The pilots shoot and hit many stormtroopers.*

HAN   —True our pilots' aim, they set us free—
              The stormtroopers surrounding us, all gone!
              Now let us hence and profit from their gift.   90
                 [*Finn watches Poe's ship.*

FINN   What skill in flying—how he moves and parries:
              First plummeting, then making bold attack.
              He dodges foes and turns them into marks,
              And thereupon doth strike with perfect aim.
              Ascending once again into the fray,   95
              He fires upon one ship and then another,

Each moment adding further to his toll.
O, unnam'd pilot, thou art friend to me!

TROOPER   [*into communicator:*] We are besieg'd—requesting air
support!

[*Exeunt stormtroopers,*
followed by Poe and Resistance pilots.

Enter REY *above, on balcony.*

REY   There is some evil presence in this wood—   100
I feel it, though I cannot see its face.
'Tis said that the best safety lies in fear,
Yet though I am afeard I feel not safe.

Enter KYLO REN *on balcony, pursuing* REY.

Suspicions all confirm'd! I am outdone!
O, how my soul is shaken and bestirr'd!   105
Shall I into this specter's bonds be trapp'd?
Avaunt—this Rey shall yet outshine thee!

[*Rey shoots at Kylo Ren.*
He deflects the shots with his lightsaber.

KYLO   —Cease!

[*He freezes her with the Force.*

The girl whose exploits fall upon mine ears.
Lest thou would feel the touch of my lightsaber,
I'd know where thou didst hide the droid I seek.   110
It seems thy tongue will not unfold the tale—
So shall I take the answer from thy mind.
Relax, give in—I'll have my wish anon.
Behold, thou hast already seen the map!

Enter a STORMTROOPER *on balcony.*

TROOPER　　　Good sir, Resistance fighters have appear'd.　　　115
　　　　　　　We need more troops if we shall win this fight.
KYLO　　　　Put thou the whole division on retreat—
　　　　　　　The droid is now of little consequence.
　　　　　　　Indeed, herein we have that which we need.
　　　　　　　　　[Kylo Ren releases Rey from the Force, and she
　　　　　　　　　　　collapses into his arms. Exeunt stormtrooper
　　　　　　　　　　　　　and Kylo Ren carrying Rey. Han, Finn,
　　　　　　　　　　　　　　　and BB-8 watch them depart.
HAN　　　　　My Ben, my son, escaping with young Rey!　　　120
　　　　　　　Confounding day, when family is turn'd
　　　　　　　To foe and stranger turn'd to family.
FINN　　　　　Rey, Rey! O, fiends, O take ye not my Rey!
　　　　　　　Nay, nay! O, Rey, my one and only friend!
BB-8　　　　　Rooq bloo, flew zzwablic roilzoon zzwaflew blis!　　　125
FINN　　　　　[*to Han:*] The scoundrel took her, fie! What shall we do?
　　　　　　　He flew and took her hence—the lass is gone.
HAN　　　　　Indeed, yet other matters fill my mind.
　　　　　　　　　[Exit Finn. Han and Chewbacca move toward
　　　　　　　　　　　an approaching ship, which lands near them.

Enter GENERAL LEIA ORGANA, *disembarking from the ship.*
Enter C-3PO *behind her, stepping between her and* HAN SOLO.

C-3PO　　　　Holla, well met, Han Solo! It is I,
　　　　　　　C-3PO. Thou, peradventure, know'st　　　130
　　　　　　　Me not, for I am lately red of arm.
　　　　　　　And dost thou see who hither hath arriv'd?—
　　　　　　　O, pray excuse me, Prin—er, General.

	Come, BB-8, and we shall let them speak.
BB-8	Blav zoonblic bloozood flitrooq blayzooz blee
	Roil flitrooh zilfreej flliblic blox zoom blee blayzood? 135
C-3PO	Yes, BB-8, I wait still for repair.

[Exeunt C-3PO and BB-8.

HAN	It pleaseth me to see thy lovely frame,
	And how thou chang'dst the fashion of thy hair.
LEIA	Yet I can see thy doublet is the same.
HAN	Nay, nay, the doublet's new, yet not so fair. 140

[Chewbacca embraces Leia.

CHEWBAC.	Egh, auugh.[14]

---

[14] *Editor's translation:* Though Han but speaks of hair and doublet style,
I thee embrace: a sight for Wookiee's eyes.

HAN   —I saw our Ben, our only son.
                    The boy himself was here a moment past.
LEIA   Let us unto th'Resistance base as one—
                    Our distant years shall be undone at last.

                                [Leia and Han embrace. Exeunt.

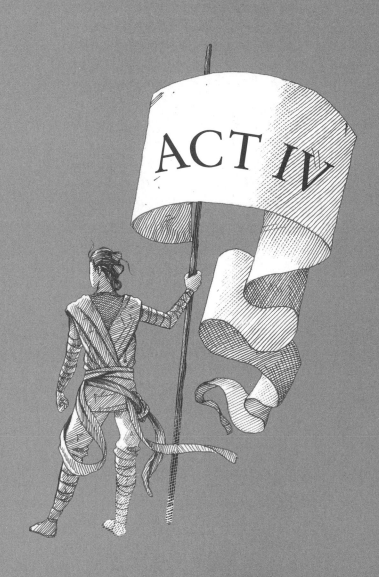

SCENE 1.

At the Resistance base on D'Qar.

Enter FINN.

FINN   Finn—even I—hath to th'Resistance come.
Its hidden base is fix'd here on D'Qar,
Yet my o'eranxious heart unfix'd doth feel.
Still Rey is missing, still her fate unknown,
Yet all around me congregate as friends   5
And celebrate a victory fulfill'd.
I would their glad festivities enjoy
Except my friend is missing and, I fear,
Perchance is gone fore'er. Let it not be,
O, Fate, kind weaver of our destinies,   10
I bid thee longer knit Rey's filament.
And what, I pray, of my next strand of life?
Shall I yet learn to fight for the Resistance?
The battle o'er on Takodana found
Me using ev'ry skill for which I train'd,   15
Yet for a noble purpose, not for evil.
It seem'd that I was born for such as this:
To work for justice, right, and honor, yea—
To face an enemy and know my cause
Was true, to help the galaxy to find   20
The peace for which it yearns with fondest hope.
Was it, though, for Resistance or for Rey
That I did fight? Or was't, perchance, for both?
Finn, let the strivings of thy troubl'd soul
Find peace in this: thou hast a calling found—   25

Be it unto a movement justified
Or to a girl whom thou dost think most fair—
Thou hast found purpose, and it is enow.

Enter POE DAMERON. *Enter* BB-8 *severally,*
rolling quickly toward POE.

Behold! 'Tis Poe, alive and flourishing!
O twist of Fate, which takes one friend from me   30
And gives another back in one fell swoop.
[*to Poe:*] Poe, Poe! 'Tis I, 'tis Finn! Thou art alive!
                    [*Poe and Finn embrace.*

POE   Perhaps it may be that my mind is wrought
To fever by the sunbeam that hangs o'er,
But I will half believe thou dost live, too!   35

FINN   What happen'd to thee after our great fall?
For certain, I was sure thou wert no more.

POE   I was, with potent force, thrown from the ship.
My spirit not awak'ning till the beam
Of moonlight struck my eyes, I woke at night.   40
There was no ship, ay, naught that I could see.

BB-8   Blav zilfroil flli flibzoon flewzoon blayblis
Bluu zzwablip blavreej zoodrooq zoomflit blee!

POE   My BB-8 reports thou sav'd him. True?
In spring of youth it was my lot to haunt   45
And seek great glory for myself, yet thou,
My friend, deserv'st it more: my mission thou
By bravery and talent did complete.
Yet—wait, forgive me, friend: is that my doublet?

FINN   I almost had forgot myself: 'tis thine.   50
Pray, take it, for thou art its rightful owner.

               [Finn begins to remove the doublet.

POE   Nay, it doth suit thee well. Keep it, 'tis thine.

              Thou art a good man, Finn: thy heart sincere,

              Thy hand true, and thine eye a kindling light:

              A rising star within th'Resistance's ranks.   55

FINN   My friend, thou hast mine utmost thanks indeed.

              Yet now I must another favor ask:

              I need thy help, Poe, in this moment fraught.

              Canst take me to thy fabl'd general?

              I've information she may sorely need.   60

POE   Indeed, we shall fly thither in a trice.

           POE *leads* FINN *into the Resistance base.*
Enter GENERAL LEIA ORGANA, HAN SOLO, C-3PO, *and various*
  RESISTANCE SOLDIERS. *Enter* R2-D2, *covered in a blanket.*

              My General Organa, pardon me

              For this brief interlude in your affairs:

              This man is Finn, who is a well-known name

              Oft utter'd in the hearing of our pilots,   65

              For he hath giv'n us aid: he'd speak with thee.

LEIA   And I with him. [*To Finn:*] Thou valor didst display,

              And bravery and honor when thou didst

              Renounce the vile First Order and escape

              With this man's life intact. Thou hast our thanks.   70

FINN   My thanks to you in turn, ma'am. 'Midst our fight

              A friend of mine was taken prisoner—

LEIA   Indeed, good Han did tell me of the girl,

              Her skill, her bravery, and her abduction.

              Apologies, good Finn: for I know what   75

              It is to lose a comrade to the foe.

	Thou hast a general's condolences.	
POE	Now to the reason why I brought him hither:	
	This Finn, as you know, once was stormtrooper—	
	No pow'r hath he of evil in himself,	80
	But hath deep knowledge of the weapon fierce	
	That did destroy the system Hosnian.	
	Finn work'd aboard the base that fir'd the blast	
	And may help us in our great hour of need.	
LEIA	We are most desp'rate for the smallest shred	85
	Of wisdom or intelligence thou hast.	
FINN	Methinks the massive base whereof we speak	
	Belike is where my friend was harshly ta'en.	
	I'd venture thither fast, and rescue her.	
LEIA	I shall do all I can to help, yet first	90
	Thou must report to us all thou dost know.	

Enter CHEWBACCA *above, on balcony, with*
DOCTOR KALONIA. *She is mending his arm.*

CHEWBAC.	Egh, auugh![15]	
KALONIA	—How passing fearful 'twas for thee.	
CHEWBAC.	Auugh, egh![16]	
KALONIA	—Indeed, thou art most brave.	
CHEWBAC.	—Egh, egh.[17]	
C-3PO	[*to Leia:*] I'm sorry, General, but it appears	
	The map from BB-8 is incomplete.	95

[15] *Editor's translation:* There were some thirty, even forty men,
And I was call'd to ward them off alone!
[16] *Editor's translation:* I fac'd the battle with a Wookiee's might—
Though I won this small scratch, they earn'd their deaths.
[17] *Editor's translation:* I'd not play mine own horn, but yea, forsooth.

From bad to worse, it matcheth no known system
Whereof we have a record. To be brief:
We've not the information that we need
To locate Master Luke where'er he is.

LEIA   How could I be so foolish to believe   100
          'Twould be so plain and simple: finding Luke
          And bringing him, then, hither to his home?

HAN   Sweet Leia—

LEIA   —Nay, do not what thou just didst.

HAN   Do what?

LEIA   —Aught.

                              [Leia walks aside.

C-3PO   [to Han:]   —Princesses are all the same.

HAN   [pursuing Leia:] I do but try to help.

LEIA   —When did that
                              work?— 105

          And speak not of the Death Star long ago!
                    [BB-8 rolls over to the blanket
                    and pulls it aside to reveal R2-D2.

BB-8   Blav zoodreej bloo flewflit blox roohzoon rooh
          Bluublee flibflir flig bleeblik blisflli flit?

C-3PO   Good BB-8, thy time thou should'st not waste—
          'Tis doubtful R2-D2 may contain   110
          The map within his backup databanks.
          I fear that R2-D2 hath remain'd
          In low-pow'r mode since Master Luke did flee.
          Bethink I he may, sadly, ne'er improve,
          Ne'er find the spark that can his light relume.   115
                    [Leia and Han speak aside.

HAN   I prithee, listen, Leia: I do know
          That when thou look'st on me, thou think'st of him.

LEIA   Imagin'st thou his mem'ry I'd forgo?
              I want him to return from his path grim.
HAN   Naught was there we could otherwise have done,   120
              To keep him on the path of light and truth.
              There was too much of Vader in our son.
LEIA   I wish'd him, then, to train with Luke, forsooth.
              Methought 'twould save him from an errant way.
              Alas, I never should have sent him hence.   125
              I thereupon lost him and thee both, yea.
HAN   Nay, say not so, it was our grieving sense:
              Like two suns that must set in their own time,
              We both return'd to th'orbit we knew best—
              I did revert unto my native clime,   130
              The tasks in which my talents are express'd.
LEIA   And so did I.
HAN   —We lost our son fore'er.

LEIA   Nay, 'twas the vile betrayer, even Snoke.
            He did seduce our son into his lair
            And bring him to the dark side, black as smoke.   135
            Forthwith we have the opportunity
            To save our son together, thou and I.

HAN   If Luke, the Jedi, could not make him see,
            And reach him in the darkness that was nigh,
            O, wherefore thinkest thou I may do so?   140

LEIA   Luke is a pow'rful Jedi, strong in will—
            Thou art his one and only father, though.
            I feel it, Han, there's light within him still.

            Enter ADMIRAL STATURA.

STATURA   My general, the news of our foes' base
            Hath just arriv'd, if you will quickly come.   145
                        [Exeunt Han, Admiral Statura,
                        Finn, Poe, droids, and soldiers.

LEIA   O, mix profound of feelings, thoughts, and news—
            My Han return'd unto my side again,
            My son reveal'd as enemy to us,
            A newfound hope we still might find dear Luke,
            A chance the vile First Order may be beaten.   150
            Some of these good reports should bring me cheer—
            Contain'd therein is cause to celebrate—
            Yet how can I e'er be content when I
            Have learn'd about my son, my boy, my Ben?
            How shall a mother learn to leave her child?   155
            To let her offspring roam, be led astray?
            How can you teach a mother to forget
            The very one she cuddl'd as a babe?

If I forget thee, son, then thou mayst hate,
If I forget thee, thou shouldst shun my voice.   160
If I forget thee, heed not my appeals,
If I forget thee, I am then no mother,
But turncoat, traitor, and a vile betrayer.
Yet this shall never happen, as thou know'st:
Though thou unto the dark side mayst have turn'd,   165
'Tis deep within thy breast, the knowledge of
Thy mother's changeless and abiding love.
I would deceive my friends ere thee forget,
I would endure the rack ere thee forget,
I would give up my life ere thee forget,   170
The galaxy would end ere thee forget.
O son, I bid thee let thy father speak,
His words fall tenderly upon thine ear,
Then listen with an open, willing heart,
Respond by spreading wide thy youthful arms,   175
And come again unto thy home with us.
Pray let it be, O soul within my son:
Feel thou our love, that three may soon be one.

                                        [Exit.

SCENE 2.

Inside Starkiller Base.

Enter Rey, *in an interrogation chair, and* Kylo Ren.

REY   Where am I?
KYLO   —Thou art welcome as my guest.
REY   Where are the others, all my comrades true?

	What hast thou done with them? Are they herein?	
KYLO	The comrades, ha! Thou meanest all the thieves,	
	The murtherers and traitors thou call'st friends?	5
	Their treachery doth mock thy loyalty,	
	Their gross dishonor doth negate thy honor.	
	Thou shalt be wholly comforted to know	
	I have no knowledge of their whereabouts.	
	Yet let us speak of them no more. Instead,	10
	'Tis thy mind that doth bring me interest:	
	Much like an open book, I look inside	
	And scan its contents like so many words.	
	Thy thoughts are clear: thou'd happ'ly see me dead.	
REY	If 'tis the story thou dost read therein,	15
	'Tis but the consequence of being hunted	
	By one who hides beneath a coward's mask.	

[Kylo Ren removes his mask.

KYLO	No craven I: I'll show my letters all,	
	Thou shalt, belike, find them a novel treat,	
	A text too heavy for thine intellect.	20
	Tell me all thou dost know about the droid.	
REY	This tale I shall unfold in simple prose:	
	A BB unit color'd white and orange,	
	A drive made of selenium withal,	
	A thermal hyperscanning vindicator—	25
KYLO	Would that thy script were sharp as thy foul tongue.	
	Pray, let me tell thee of thy literature:	
	The droid doth hold a navigating chart—	
	We have a fragment—'twas recover'd from	
	The archives of the Empire virtuous—	30
	Yet we require the piece that doth remain.	
	Thou somehow didst convince the errant droid	

To show the map to thee, a scavenger—
Of lowly birth and even lower class.
Thou canst see, by this knowledge I've obtain'd,   35
That I'd become the author of thy fate.
I shall procure what I desire from thee
And thy weak mind, pathetic as it is.

[Kylo Ren uses the Force
to extract thoughts from Rey's mind.

I see the narrative that thou dost pen:
How sad thou art, in misery enwrapp'd—   40
Thou art alone, of leaving most afeard.
At night, thou art so desperate to sleep.
Within thy mind an ocean, and an isle
Plac'd in the ocean's vast expanse—I see't.
Han Solo: he is in thy mind as well.   45
To thee he seemeth like the father whom
Thou ne'er didst know. Hear thou my words most true:
The man, I'll warrant, would but disappoint.
Thy chronicle is tragic in the height.

REY   Avaunt, thou knave! Get hence—close thou my book!   50
KYLO   Yet 'tis a tome whose end I long to see,
Although it is a simple one to scan:
I know thou hast laid eyes upon the chart.
'Tis in thy head, and thou shalt give it me.
Anon it shall be mine. Be not afraid,   55
I feel the strange connection 'twixt us, too.
[*Aside:*] Her mind is far more strong than I bethought,
A volume of some weight, I do confess.

REY   Naught shall I show thee.
KYLO   —This remains to see.
REY   [*aside:*] I sense wherein he entereth my mind—   60

Perchance I may his ruse turn back on him.
The man hath entered th'archive of my mind;
Mayhap I may assail his library.
[*To Kylo Ren:*] Yet even as thou read'st, thou shalt be
                                read:
Thou art afraid thou ne'er shalt be as strong   65
As he thou dost admire: the Sith, Darth Vader.
Ha! Ope again, for I would fain read more!
               [*Exit Rey as Kylo Ren makes his way
                         to the assembly room.*

KYLO   Nay, nay, it cannot be. It must not be!
How did this wretched girl of simple stock
Refocus my direction of the Force?   70
Have I grown feeble, soft, or witless? Nay!
She turn'd the trick on me with seeming ease.
Perforce the lady is instinctively
Strong in the Force, though she may know it not.
This failure, still, is unacceptable,   75
An errant step along my path of dark.
I shall consult wise Supreme Leader Snoke,
Confessing my mistake and her resolve.

Enter SUPREME LEADER SNOKE *and* GENERAL HUX.

SNOKE   Already I sense wherefore thou hast come:
The scavenger resisted thee. But how?   80
HUX   [*aside:*] Alack, dissembling and unworthy wretch!
KYLO   Forgive me, she is gifted with the Force,
Far abler than she knoweth.
SNOKE   —And the droid?
HUX   'Twas Ren's belief it had no further worth—

He thought the girl was ev'rything to us,   85
The be-all and the end-all. Consequently,
The droid, belike, is with our enemies.
'Tis possible the map is in their hands.

SNOKE   The weak Resistance must then be destroy'd
Ere they've the chance to contact Skywalker.   90
We have no time for patience, by my troth.

HUX   We know the setting of their hidden base—
Their vessel of reconnaissance we track'd
Unto the system of Ileenium.

SNOKE   'Tis well—thou, Hux, hath not fail'd me herein.   95
They shall be crush'd and finally destroy'd.
Prepare the weapon for our swift attack.

HUX   It shall be done at once, and with delight.
                              [Exit General Hux.

KYLO   My Supreme Leader, I can get the map—
The girl I may o'ercome if you'll guide me.   100

SNOKE   If what thou say'st about the girl is true,
That she hath special powers in the Force,
Bring her to me, and we shall ope her mind.
                              [Exeunt.

Enter REY, *in the interrogation chair.*
Enter a STORMTROOPER, *aside.*

REY   'Twas passing strange, what happen'd unto me:
I turn'd the villain's trick upon himself.   105
Such pow'r I never knew I did possess—
Perchance 'twas but an accident of fortune
Or some impermanent coincidence.
Still, I am most intrigued by what hath pass'd:

Some miracle, or something else entire?   110
Is't possible I have some pow'r unknown?
Bethink I on it, and it seems absurd;
Lo, I must foolish be to think it so.
Extends the Force to people such as I?
Is our vast galaxy so spacious that   115
Both rich and poor alike may know its pow'r?
Yet if the Force is as I once was told—
That which surrounds and binds us all as one—
How could it inaccessible remain,
E'en to a humble person as myself?   120
Forsooth, the Force hath room enow for all.
O, would that it were so—my hope fulfill'd!
Rey, then, could be far more than scavenger,
Could be a warrior or Jedi Knight!
Excitement doth o'erwhelm me at such thoughts.   125
Well may I put this notion to the test:
Aside there is a stormtrooper who doth
Stand vigilant 'gainst an attempt to flee.
Shall I here try to call upon the Force
To use a mind trick of which I've heard tell?   130
Yea, I shall try: what evil could befall?
Lo, stormtrooper, I bid thee hear my call:
E'en now you shall remove these strong restraints,
Depart the cell, and leave the door ajar.

TROOPER   Didst thou speak? And what was it thou didst say?   135
Now wherefore wouldst thou speak? I do not know.
E'en such a one as thee speak unto me?
Lo, thou art surely mad. Canst hear my words?
Revil'd and hated scum, thou art too bold.
Avaunt! If thou must speak, then make it plain: 140

Grant me to hear again the words thou spok'st!
REY E'en now you shall release me from my bonds,
Depart the cell, and leave the door ajar.
TROOPER I'll tighten up thy bonds, make thee a specter.
REY [*aside:*] Pray, clear thy thoughts now, Rey, and
concentrate. 145
[*To stormtrooper:*] E'en now you shall release me from
my bonds,
Depart the cell, and leave the door ajar.
TROOPER E'en now I shall release thee from thy bonds,
Depart the cell, and leave the door ajar.
[The stormtrooper begins to leave.
REY Indeed, thy weapon thou shalt also drop. 150
TROOPER Indeed, my weapon I shall also drop.
[He drops his weapon and exits.
REY I wonder at this strange ability:
Why should the Force be mine, thus to employ?
This power was not bidden, I did call
It not, did seek it not, did want it not. 155
Yet still it cometh: O, what mystery.
[Exit.

Enter KYLO REN.

KYLO What's this? How hath she vanish'd into air?
Where is the girl I left but moments past?
What vast incompetence or trickery—
Why do we utilize these stormtroopers? 160
O, loggerheaded, dismal-dreaming louts!
*[Kylo Ren brandishes his lightsaber and begins
to destroy the room.*

Goatish idle-headed canker-blossoms!
Would that the one responsible for this—
Or, rather, irresponsible for this—
Were here to feel the full vent of mine anger!   165
I'd beat him until he were wholly senseless,
I'd hang him until he for mercy begg'd,
I'd show to him my hot lightsaber's edge—
O, out upon them, may they all be slain!

Enter GENERAL HUX *and various* TECHNICIANS *above, on balcony.*

HUX   Begin the charging of the weapon, sirrah.   170
TECH   'Tis done: the weapon chargeth even now.
HUX   The pitiful Resistance ends today,
          For we shall make our strike without delay.
                                        [Exeunt.

SCENE 3.

At the Resistance base on D'Qar.

Enter CHORUS.

CHORUS   The cruel First Order doth begin its plan
          To end th'Resistance in a flash of light.
          Meanwhile, upon D'Qar, our heroes scan
          For some advantage that may help their plight.
                                        [Exit Chorus.

Enter GENERAL LEIA ORGANA, HAN SOLO, CHEWBACCA,
FINN, POE DAMERON, ADMIRAL ACKBAR, ADMIRAL

STATURA, MAJOR BRANCE, MAJOR EMATT, SNAP WEXLEY,
C-3PO, *and various* RESISTANCE SOLDIERS.

POE   The scan from the reconnaissance report   5
                That Snap hath here provided doth confirm
                What Finn hath told us: this new base is like
                Unto some vicious, strange, proud evening star,
                More powerful than ever we have seen.
SNAP   If I have read the shrewd reports aright,   10
                Methinks they have created, spitefully,
                A hyper lightspeed weapon, which resides
                Within the planet's very nucleus.
BRANCE   'Tis then a laser cannon?
SNAP   —We've no names
                By which to call a weapon of this size: 15
                It passeth all the boundaries of speech,
                The faculty of ev'ry language, e'en
                The power of a poet's way with words.
EMATT   An that thou dost not overstate, it is
                Belike another Death Star, help us all.   20
                      [Poe projects a model of the Death Star next to
                         a model of Starkiller Base, which is far larger.
POE   Ah, would that it were so, good major. Pray,
                Behold the model, sir: Starkiller Base
                Is of a magnitude beyond our fears.
                In visions of the dark night I had ne'er
                Imagin'd such an awful sight as this.   25
                No Death Star, this; 'tis like a Death Star system.
HAN   So 'tis a bigger weapon. Is that all?
                Place we such emphasis on size alone?
ACKBAR   How can so large a weapon power'd be?

	It would require vast energy to sap.	30
FINN	It useth all the power of a star:	
	The weapon is full chargèd whilst the sun	
	Doth disappear. The thing is fiendish, sirs.	
LEIA	Alas, our recent news reports the same:	
	The rank First Order charges it e'en now,	35
	Our system next upon its list of death.	
C-3PO	Sans our Republic's fleet, I fear we're doom'd.	
HAN	How shall we then destroy the awful thing?	
	Doth history not give us present hope?	
	There ever is some way to make defeat	40
	Of that which doth seem undefeatable!	
	O, brave Resistance fighters, be ye brave—	
	This day is call'd the feast of Odan-Urr.	
	They that outlive this day, and come safe home,	
	Will stand a-tiptoe when this day is nam'd,	45
	And rouse them at the name of Odan-Urr.	
	They that shall live this day, and see old age,	
	Will yearly on the vigil feast their neighbors	
	And say, "Tomorrow's the centenary."	
	Then will they strip their sleeves and show their scars	50
	And say, "These wounds I had on Odan's day."	
	Old folk forget; yet all shall be forgot,	
	But they'll remember with advantages	
	What feats they did that day. Then shall our names,	
	Familiar in their mouth as household words—	55
	Sweet General Leia and Adm'ral Ackbar,	
	Poe Dameron and Ematt, Finn and Snap—	
	Be in their flowing cups freshly remember'd.	
	This story shall each parent teach their child;	
	And Odan-Urr's feast day shall ne'er go by,	60

From this day to the end of th'universe,
But we in it shall be remember'd, too—
We few, we happy few, we band of comrades;
For they today who shed their blood with me
Shall be my comrades; be they ne'er so vile,   65
This day shall gentle their condition, yea.
So be ye not afeard, my friends, be strong—
'Twill be our finest victory to date,
This grand Starkiller shall be our kill yet!

LEIA   My Han! Brave man, would thou and I alone,   70
              Without more help, could fight this present battle!

STATURA   Indeed—thy words inspire my thoughts again.
              For that amount of pow'r to be contain'd,
              The base must have a thermal oscillator!
                                    *[Finn points to a section of
                              the projected model of Starkiller Base.*

FINN   Forsooth, thou hast it right: it is therein.   75
              In Precinct Forty-Seven, by my troth.

STATURA   Methinks if th'oscillator were destroy'd,
              It may the core destabilize and, then—
              If Fortune smiles upon our bold Resistance—
              Undo the weapon fully.

EMATT   —E'en the planet.   80

POE   To seek for treasure in the jewel'd skies
              We'll fly, and strike the oscillator with
              Our strongest and our fiercest armaments.
              Our pilots and our ships are strong and true,
              Prepar'd to fly upon the moment when   85
              Our noble general doth say the word.

ACKBAR   Let us not be o'erhasty in our plan,
              But think of ev'ry consequence we may.

                What of the strong defenses they have set?

                Their shields, belike, may give a mighty slap.   90

HAN   We'll undertake to bring their rough shields down.

                [*To Finn:*] Thou wert employ'd thereat. What dost

                                        thou think?

FINN   [*aside:*] My confidence herein doth sorely lack—

                To save sweet Rey, though, I must sound most firm.

                [*To Han:*] I am most confident I'll make it so.   95

HAN   This lad's a goodly sort, I'll warrant, ha!

FINN   Yet further: to undo the shields I must

                Be thereupon, e'en on the planet's face,

                For only thence can their strong shields be dropp'd.

HAN   We shall convey thee thither in the *Falcon.*   100

LEIA   O, man both quick to move and slow to think,

                Is this another unwise Solo scheme?

                I prithee, how?

HAN   —Mine answer thou'dst not like—

                My thinking being far too slow for thee,

                My mind shall keep its private counsel, ma'am.   105

POE   'Tis settl'd, then: the shields shall be destroy'd,

                The oscillator devastated quick,

                Their weapon thereby utterly demolish'd.

                Their years of hatred shall have been forgot

                Within the battle of a minute. Go!   110

                Let us arise and venture forth anon—

                For the Resistance and for victory!

                      [*Exeunt Poe, Admiral Ackbar, Admiral*

                          Statura, Major Brance, Major Ematt,

                    Snap Wexley, C-3PO, and Resistance soldiers.

                    Han, Chewbacca, and Finn make preparations

                          to leave as Leia watches, aside.

HAN	Bold Chewie, check our ship's capacitor;
	We fly as soon as shall be possible.
	And Finn, I bid thee take abundant care 115
	With those metallic spheres—they do explode.
FINN	Now, after I have held them, thou so say'st?
	Thou'dst fix me in a Wampa's company,
	And only later tell me it hath fangs!

[Exeunt Chewbacca and Finn.

| LEIA | [approaching:] 'Twas always so: however much we |

fought, 120

	To watch thee leave did fill me with remorse.
HAN	'Twas wherefore I have other places sought:
	That thou wouldst miss my heart in time's due course.

[They embrace.

LEIA	Ay, verily, it work'd: I miss'd thee so.
HAN	'Twas not all bad—our past, our history? 125
	Full many moments e'en, methinks, did glow.
LEIA	They still do glow within my memory.
HAN	Some habits of our lives shall ne'er be chang'd.
LEIA	Indeed, thou still art troubler of my days,
	The one who keeps my spirit disarrang'd. 130
	O, Han, if on our son thou chanc'st to gaze,
	I prithee, bring him home with thee again:
	Then two may yet be three: thou, I, and Ben.

[Exeunt.

SCENE 4.

Inside Starkiller Base.

Enter KYLO REN *and* STORMTROOPERS.

TROOPER 1	Sir, sensors trigger'd—hangar 718.
	Our troops do scan the area e'en now.
	We shall yet find the wily, cunning girl.
KYLO	'Tis well. She doth begin to test her pow'rs,
	I'll wager that the longer she's unfound, 5
	The stronger and more daring she becomes.
	Thus must we quickly find her where she hides.

[Exit Kylo Ren.

TROOPER 1	The man is in a frightful mood today.
TROOPER 2	Indeed—this Ren is not a happy sort,
	E'er storming 'round the base with angry steps, 10
	Destroying our equipment in his rage,
	And threatening our troops with punishment.
	How he reminds me of another one
	I knew within the Empire long ago.
TROOPER 1	I almost had forgot that thou hast serv'd 15
	Within the Empire many ages hence.
	'Tis what, some three or four full decades now?
	Say, what hath chang'd in th'intervening years?
TROOPER 2	Far more than thou imaginest, I'll wager.
TROOPER 1	Indeed?
TROOPER 2	—Indeed. When I began my job, 20
	I did report unto a dreadful man
	All garb'd in black, his face hid 'neath a mask,
	With vicious moods and lightsaber of red.
TROOPER 1	Hath Kylo Ren been all this time alive?

	Methought he was far younger. Is he not?	25
TROOPER 2	Nay, 'twas not Kylo Ren, but one Darth Vader.	
TROOPER 1	I know him not, though I have heard the name.	
	What of the base whereon thou wert employ'd?	
TROOPER 2	A vast, forbidding base form'd in a sphere,	
	Which some mistook for some celestial body.	30
	It hous'd more soldiers than most armies boast.	
	Its purpose was to crush a planet whole.	
TROOPER 1	Starkiller Base existed even then?	
TROOPER 2	Nay, 'twas the Death Star. Wholly different.	
TROOPER 1	I see. And who were then thine enemies?	35
TROOPER 2	A group of young and naïve ingenues:	
	One who was rais'd upon a planet sparse,	
	Burnt by the sun and fill'd with sandy dunes.	
TROOPER 1	Yet wait—the fugitives for whom we seek?	
	Thou speakest of the girl from dour Jakku?	40
	Is't possible we've search'd for them this long?	
TROOPER 2	Nay, nay, a group dissimilar completely,	
	A set of naughty youngsters now grown old.	
TROOPER 1	What was the oddest place they were pursu'd?	
TROOPER 2	Ah, let me think. It must have been the bar—	45
	A strange cantina in a lonely place,	
	Fill'd with such varied aliens and beasts	
	As thou could ne'er see in a hundred systems.	
TROOPER 1	Forsooth, I know the place! We were just there,	
	On Takodana—Maz's castle, 'twas—	50
	Where we fought the Resistance th'other day.	
TROOPER 2	Nay, nay, this was near forty years ago,	
	When one old Jedi fool'd me mightily	
	With Jedi mind trick nasty and unfair.	
	He said the droids wherewith he travel'd were	55

	Not those same droids that I was looking for.
TROOPER 1	And yet they were?
TROOPER 2	—Alas, I do confess.

TROOPER 2
                     —Alas, I do confess.
I do regret the terrible mistake,
For which I've fac'd more jests than I can count.

TROOPER 1 What of the droids thou sought? What were they like? 60

TROOPER 2 One of the droids was colorful and domed—
It spoke in beeps and squeaks most insolent.

TROOPER 1 Indeed? The BB unit we do seek?

TROOPER 2 Nay, friend—another droid from scope to wheels.

TROOPER 1 'Tis clear life long ago was different, 65
And not at all the same as modern times.
I envy thine experience, my comrade—
Thou hast seen so much of our galaxy.

TROOPER 2 So shalt thou, an thou work'st as long as me!
Fate ever weaveth new experience— 70
No thread the same, unique in ev'ry stitch,
And ev'ry episode both fresh and rich!

                     [Exeunt.

SCENE 5.

In the Millennium Falcon *and on Starkiller Base.*

Enter HAN SOLO, CHEWBACCA, *and* FINN *inside the*
Millennium Falcon, *flying at lightspeed toward Starkiller Base.*

FINN How shall we penetrate the planet's surface?
I'll warrant thou hast figur'd out the plan.

HAN The shields of the First Order do maintain
A fractional refresh rate, which doth mean

	Aught that doth travel slower than lightspeed	5
	Shall ne'er get through. Yet that shall not be us,
	If thou dost catch the message I relay.

FINN   Thou plann'st to landing make at full lightspeed?

CHEWBAC.   Egh![18]

HAN   —Chewie be prepar'd. Now, comrade, now!

Pray, disengage, or we shall run aground.   10

FINN   O, pull'd most suddenly from lightspeed's thrust—

We hit the ground, the trees, the surface all,

How we are thrown about, like featherweights!

'Tis madness, what thy plan doth foist on us!

HAN   Though this be madness, yet there's method in't.   15

CHEWBAC.   Auugh![19]

HAN   —Yea, I am a'pulling up! Tut, tut!

CHEWBAC.   Egh, auugh![20]

HAN   —Nay, higher and we shall be seen!

[*The* Millennium Falcon *crashes to a halt on the*
snowy surface of Starkiller Base.

Enter KYLO REN *and* TROOPER 1 *above, on balcony.*

TROOPER 1   She was not found in hangar 718,

Yet ev'ry trooper stayeth on alert.

Methinks the scheming girl shall be found soon.   20

KYLO   Lock down, I prithee, ev'ry hangar now.

Belike she shall attempt to steal a ship.

If she doth make escape, I am undone,

---

[18] *Editor's translation:* For fortitude, not prudence, are we known!
[19] *Editor's translation:* O, captain of insanity: pull up!
[20] *Editor's translation:* Methinks at least a little higher, Han!

    My search for Skywalker must start anew.
    [*Aside:*] What is this newfound presence that I sense? 25
    Han Solo, come unto Starkiller Base.
    The fool—what means he by his presence here?
          [Exeunt Kylo Ren and Trooper 1.

FINN   [*to Han and Chewbacca:*] My stomach is reliev'd to feel
              the ground,
    Its sure and steady presence underfoot—
    Far better than the rocking, hurtling ship. 30
    Come hither, to the flooding tunnel spot:
    There shall we first make entrance to the base.

HAN   Thou must, as one who was a stormtrooper,
    Have knowledge vast of this enormous base.
    What was thy task when thou didst work herein? 35

FINN   It was the pungent field of sanitation.

HAN   Thou art the grim First Order's garbage man?
    The man who took out trash for trashy men?
    How then dost thou know how to stop the shields?

FINN   I shall confess to thee: I do not know.
    My function here is to retrieve sweet Rey; 40
    The rest, friend, we shall make up as we go.

HAN   Our mission doth rely on our success—
    Our comrades do rely on our success—
    The galaxy relies on our success! 45

FINN   Good Solo, all shall yet be fine, methinks.
    We shall employ the Force in all its might!

HAN   Thou knowest nothing of the mighty Force
    Or how it worketh, folly-laden youth.

CHEWBAC. Egh![21]

---

[21] *Editor's translation:* Can we press on? My fur is getting chill'd!

HAN   —Thou art cold? Eh, Wookiee?
FINN   —Follow on!   50

Enter GENERAL HUX *and a* TECHNICIAN *above, on balcony.*

HUX   I bid thee, sirrah, make thy full report.
TECH   The weapon shall be charg'd in fifteen minutes!
               Then we may strike the weak Resistance base.
HUX   Yet fifteen minutes and our work's complete,
               Yea, fifteen minutes for our rise to come,   55
               But fifteen minutes left for the Resistance:
               These fifteen minutes cannot be too swift.
                        [Exeunt General Hux and technician.
                        Han, Chewbacca, and Finn enter the base.
HAN   The longer we do spend our time hereon,
               The less that lady luck doth smile on us.
               O, luck, if thou wert ever lady to begin,   60
               O, luck, be thou a lady in this base.
               Now, Bigness, what is thy plan for the shields?
               Heav'n help us, thou still art the leader here.
FINN   No plan is fix'd, but thoughts begin to fly.
               I'd find one with the right authority,   65
               A foe with top credentials in this base.

Enter CAPTAIN PHASMA.

          This is the focal point of my idea—
          She is the perfect foil for my design.
                      [Finn motions to Han and Chewbacca,
                        and they overtake Captain Phasma.
          Dost thou remember me, phantasm foul?

PHASMA	A nickel wit: FN-2187. 70
FINN	Nay, nay, now I am Finn. A-ha! 'Tis Finn! I am in charge of thee—I am in charge! Finn is in charge, and leads the charge, and doth Charge thee to feel the current of my charge!
HAN	Pray, Bigness, calm—charge down thy batteries. 75 Thou hast the upper hand, but bear it well.
FINN	Now follow, Captain Phasma. We have work.

     [Finn, Han, and Chewbacca walk Captain Phasma
                    to the control room, guarding her.

Enter REY, *on balcony.*

REY	I broke my bonds, but am not wholly free. The chair, the cell, those have I left behind, But I must find a way to steal a ship, 80

Remove myself from this bleak house wherein
Our foes reside, and then return unto
Our mutual friends, wherever they may be.
Rey would be free! Not part, but all of her,
I have great expectations of escape,   85
But have not heard the chimes of liberty.
The battle of my life doth turn and twist—
It seems 'tis a tale of two citizens—
One Rey on copper fields of drab Jakku,
One Rey who shares hard times with the Resistance.   90
Ah, what the dickens shall my future hold?
                                        [Exit Rey.

FINN   Thou hast one option, else I'll happ'ly fire
            The helmet from thy pate: force down the shields.

PHASMA   Thy faults are sterling in their dreadfulness.

FINN   Pray, do it. [*She deactivates the shields.*] Solo, should
                                        this find success,   95
            We'll have but little time for filching Rey.

HAN   Fear not, lad, we shall not sans her depart.

PHASMA   It seemeth mercury doth quickly rise
            If thou hast grown to be so passing ill
            That thou think'st 'twill be simple. My bold troops   100
            Shall storm this block and kill you all anon.
            Thou e'er wert weak and never shall succeed.

FINN   Nay, fiend, thou art mistaken. [*To Han:*] What of her?
            How shall we of this enemy dispose?

HAN   Is there a trash compactor?

FINN   —Aye, my friend.   105

HAN   'Twill show the justice of the galaxy:
            One thing is certain: she shall thinner be.
                                        [Exeunt.

SCENE 6.

At the Resistance base on D'Qar and in the air above Starkiller Base.

Enter GENERAL LEIA ORGANA, ADMIRAL STATURA, C-3PO,
and an OFFICER *above, on balcony. Enter* POE DAMERON,
SNAP WEXLEY, NIEN NUNB, YOLO ZIFF, *and* ELLO ASTY *in their ships.*

OFFICER	My general, the shields are down at last,
	And we may undertake our bold offense!
C-3PO	O, thank the maker!
LEIA	—Han achiev'd the feat!
	Send in the pilots to begin th'assault.
STATURA	Give Poe authority to make attack.

5

OFFICER	Black leader, to thy sublights. On thy call!

[Exeunt Leia, Admiral Statura,
C-3PO, and officer.

POE	Thy words I do receive with joy and hope!
	Now is the time for Poe to make his mark—
	I dwelt alone within a world of moan,
	And my soul was a stagnant tide until
	I met the brave Resistance and did learn
	The purpose of my life, profound and firm:
	To use my skills to be a pilot brave
	And true unto a cause I champion.
	The principle for which I learn'd to live,
	I would most happ'ly perish for, as well.
	[*To other pilots:*] Now are we almost in the range to
	strike—
	Aim on the oscillator powerful.
	Pray, mark the target in its center spot,

10

15

                    And hit it forcefully with all ye have!   20
YOLO   I drop from lightspeed even now, Black Leader.
SNAP   Approaching target now!
NIEN   —Ungate-oh!

        Enter GENERAL HUX *and* COLONEL DATOO *aside, in base.*

HUX   The cry is still "They come!" Our base's strength
            Will laugh a siege to scorn! Yea, let them come!
            Dispatch our squadrons fierce.
DATOO   —Yea, general.   25
                    [Exeunt General Hux and Colonel Datoo.
SNAP   Direct hit!
ELLO   —Yet no damage doth result.
            The oscillator is, I fear, too strong.
POE   We must continue with our strike—keep on!
            Another bomb attack we make anon.
            Through all the flimsy things we see at once,   30
            Let us remember this: when that the sun
            Doth disappear from sight, the weapon is
            Prepar'd to fire again. Yet whilst there's light,
            We have a chance to win the day, my friends.
            We must press on toward the victory,   35
            Maintaining our endeavors in the field.
            But soft, behold our newfound company—
            TIE fighters rising from the enemy!
                            [Exeunt all, in confusion.

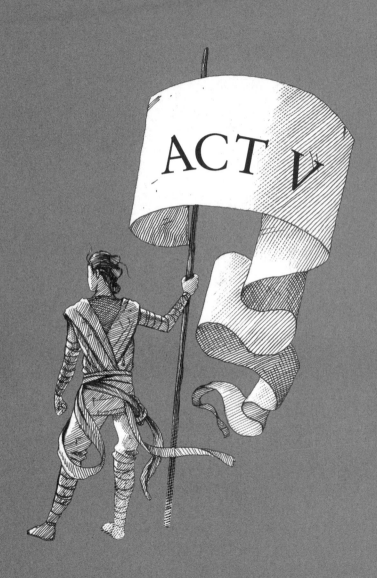

SCENE 1.

Inside Starkiller Base.

Enter Han Solo, Chewbacca, *and* Finn.

FINN   The blast door by these charges can be fell'd.
                I shall draw fire, but need your cover, too.
HAN   Say truly: art thou ready for this fight?

Enter Rey *aside, climbing on a wall to escape.*

FINN   Ha, nay! Thou seest my face and know the truth,
                I am of this encounter terrified.   5
                A stronger influence works on me, though:

My longing to discover my kind friend.
The shields are down, thus to our final task:
We'll find sweet Rey and take her from this place,
Though troopers follow nearly at our backs—   10
We must be ready for that consequence.
There is, nearby, an access tunnel for—
    [Han motions toward Rey with his chin.
What is this motion that o'ertakes thy face?
Say wherefore dost thou jut thy chin just so?
Is this some signal known to smuggler folk?   15
Or, senses fled, thou frantic hast become?
Dost fly to madness and begin to twitch?
I stand here, planning for the next endeavor,
And thou, so steep'd in fear, can but convulse?

HAN   I prithee, Bigness, stop thy mouth and look.   20
Talk less, smile more; throw not away thy shot.
    [Finn turns and sees Rey.
Rey, art thou well?

REY   —Indeed.

HAN   —O, thank'd be Fate.

FINN   What happen'd to thee? Wert thou foully harm'd?
If thou wert hurt, I vengeance shall require.

REY   No injury to speak of, by my troth.   25
I'll warrant, though, it is thy turn to speak:
Finn, wherefore hast thou come unto this place?

FINN   We made return for thee.

REY   *[aside:]*   —O, blessèd words,
Which I so many years have long'd to hear,
Though not from this mouth in this circumstance.   30
Still, how they sweetly ring within mine ears!

CHEWBAC.   Egh, auugh![22]

FINN   —What did the fine Chewbacca say?

REY   He doth report 'twas thy idea to come
          And rescue me. Ne'er have I such friend had.

                              [Rey and Finn embrace.
          My many thanks.

FINN   —How didst thou flee thy bonds?   35

REY   I cannot say, and thou wouldst not believe.
          Some other time I'd tell thee ev'rything.

HAN   While this fond scene is touching in th'extreme,
          Perhaps escape anon, embrace hereafter?
          To hug a lov'd one is a sacred thing—   40
          Far better, though, if both remain alive.

                    [They run from the base outside into the snow.
          Alas, our friends are troubl'd in their task.
          Behold our X-wings, flying o'er the ground:
          They have arriv'd in safety, only to
          Be doggedly pursued by enemies.   45
          I see one fall e'en now—Furillo's ship,
          If still mine older eyes do see aright.
          The ground fire coupled with the vile TIE fighters
          May be too much. I see they have not yet
          The oscillator damag'd or destroy'd.   50
          In short: we cannot leave, we've more to do.
          Chewbacca hath a bag of jolly treats—
          Explosives that shall work their alchemy
          Upon this base. I say, 'tis time to use them.
          Methinks it is the best help we can proffer.   55

---

[22] *Editor's translation:* Thou shalt be giv'n more reason for surprise:
   'Twas Finn's design to come and rescue thee.

Enter GENERAL LEIA ORGANA, C-3PO,
and an OFFICER *above, on balcony.*

OFFICER   Good general, have you seen this report?
           Two more X-wings have fallen—half our fleet
           Hath by the cruel First Order been destroy'd.
           What shall we do? Is't time to sound retreat?
C-3PO   Their weapon shall be fully charg'd in but   60
           Ten minutes. O, what pain to see this day!
           'Twould take a miracle to save us now.
                           [Exeunt Leia, C-3PO, and officer.
HAN   *[to Rey:]* We'll enter to the oscillator if
           Thou canst undo th'electric doors and earn
           Us access to the grand control room.
REY   —Yea,   65
           The circuitry herein is plain enow.
           I'll warrant it shall open in a trice—
           We'll do the deed and follow after ye.
                           [Rey and Finn enter a maintenance hatch.
           A life of scavenging upon Jakku—
           Of learning all the inward parts of ships,   70
           Becoming too familiar with their guts,
           And seeing their construction and their wires—
           Prepar'd me fully for this moment here.
           The complicated system of electrics
           Are like a puzzle longing to be solv'd—   75
           E'en as I look upon it I can see
           The pattern and the key that lies therein.
           I'd ne'er believe I would be thankful for
           The many years I spent at foraging.
           Yet here, they testify their boundless worth: 80

My past informs and guides my present moment
And still may lead my future, come what may.
    [Rey manipulates the controls and the doors open.
                                    Exeunt Rey and Finn.

HAN   She doth the knotty task with seeming ease;
             The knowledge of the girl is true.

CHEWBAC.   —Egh, auugh.[23]

HAN   The doors are open. Let us, then, proceed.   85
             Pray, let us lay a charge at ev'ry column.

CHEWBAC.   Egh, egh.[24]

HAN   —Thou hast it better, friend, than I;
             A vertical assault is more complete.
             Thou shalt ascend above and lay the bombs.
             Meanwhile, I shall with charges go below.   90
             Take thou the detonator with great care,
             And we shall meet once more upon this spot.
                          [Han and Chewbacca separate
                                and begin setting explosives.

                Enter KYLO REN *and* STORMTROOPERS.

KYLO   I bid ye, find the foes who come herein.
             My senses tell me they do hide e'en now.
                          [Stormtroopers search the area.

HAN   [*aside:*] My son. There doth he stand and walk and
                                            live, 95

---

[23] *Editor's translation:* Then why have we not offer'd her a job?
[24] *Editor's translation:* Nay, listen to my counsel in this instance:
    This chamber is so wondrous tall and broad—
    Should we not separate and lay a charge
    Both up above and down below as well?

I cannot look on him and see a foe—
No enemy walks there, but my sweet boy.
O, how the memories o'ertake my soul:
The news that was deliver'd unto us,
The happy expectation of a child,   100
The introduction unto parenthood,
The pure and perfect infant whom we held
Whilst he did smile and coo, e'en when he was
Mewling and puking in his mother's arms—
No matter: he was flawless in our eyes.   105
O, how he alter'd e'en a smuggler's life!
I learn'd to be the pilot of a cradle,
To steer the ast'roid field of fatherhood,
To sing a roughhewn scoundrel's lullaby,
To change soil'd clothes as fast as lightspeed's pace. 110
When young, his smile could light a darken'd room,
He play'd with zeal, with fervent joy and glee,
Approach'd the world with wonder and delight,
Which—seeing ev'rything through his two eyes—
Instructed me and Leia thus to see.   115
His mother and I both were thunderstruck,
In love with our dear child, in love with life,
In love with th'myst'ry of the galaxy
That brought such tender happiness to us.
Full many nights we'd lie awake and watch   120
Him as he slept, in silent adoration,
E'en when we were exhausted to the bone:
A newfound parent's privilege and folly.
Ne'er could we think, those ages now gone hence,
That I would face him on a battlefield,   125
That he'd be counted with our enemies,

That he would choose to talk with evil men,
That he should come to hate his given name.
O, Solo soul that learn'd to sing duet,
Then learn'd a trio melody so fine,   130
Be strong but loving in this moment. [*To Kylo Ren:*]
                                    Ben!

> [*Kylo Ren turns to see Han Solo.*
> *Chewbacca and the stormtroopers freeze,*
> *watching the encounter.*

KYLO   Han Solo. Long have I awaited this.

Enter REY *and* FINN *above, on balcony, observing the scene.*

HAN   Remove thy mask; thou need'st it not with me.
KYLO   What dost thou think shall be reveal'd beneath,
            Were I to take it off?
HAN   —My son's dear face.   135

> [*Kylo Ren removes his mask.*

            [*Aside:*] A boy no longer, now a man complete.
            The shadows of his boyhood I can see,
            Yet hidden deep within his manly visage.
KYLO   Thy son is gone. The boy was weak, indeed,
            Too soft and foolish, like his father is.   140
            He was an errant and misguided child—
            I did, therefore, destroy thy son with pride.
HAN   Nay, 'tis what Snoke desires that you believe,
            Yet it hath not the ring of truth. My son,
            My dear and only son, he liveth still,   145
            And thou art he, and he, my son, is thou.
            The two of you, who art one, both are lov'd.
KYLO   Thou speakest like a jester and a fool,

	Whereas my leader Snoke is passing wise.	
HAN	Snoke is not wise—the word is devious.	150
	He doth but use thee for thy mighty pow'r.	
	Once he obtains what he seeks, thereupon	
	Shall he destroy thee—verily, thou know'st.	
KYLO	[*aside:*] How these words sting, and how my soul doth	
	yearn	
	To feel, once more, the favor of my father.	155
	I must be strong, remembering the truth	
	To which I have been led by Leader Snoke	
	And not the vain, false comfort offer'd by	
	The one whom I did once a father call.	
	O, let my actions here be firm and sure,	160
	Rejecting what he'd proffer unto me	
	And thus embracing darkness. [*To Han:*] 'Tis too late.	
HAN	Nay, never. Come, return unto thy home.	
	We miss thy gentle presence in our lives.	
	'Tis not too late—'tis ne'er too late, my son.	165
KYLO	I do confess that I am torn asunder.	
	From all this pain I fain would be set free.	
	I know what I must do, yet fear I've not	
	The strength to make it so. O, wilt thou help?	
	[Kylo Ren reaches to hand Han his lightsaber.	
HAN	Of course, whate'er thou wishest, my sweet boy—	170
	Thou bring'st and e'er did bring me such great joy.	
KYLO	[*aside:*] Beyond the chamber dies the light outside,	
	An 'twere the light within my very soul—	
	Thus in my core doth darkness reign at last.	
	[Kylo Ren turns on his lightsaber	
	and runs Han through.	
HAN	My son, whose face is still so dear to me—	175

O, how I see thy mother still in thee.

Dear Leia, who did love this scoundrel so,

I've fail'd thee, could not save our boy from woe.

Mount, mount, my soul! Thy seat is up on high,

Whilst my gross flesh sinks downward, here to die.   180

[Han Solo dies.

KYLO   My thanks, old man, thou giv'st me what I need.

CHEWBAC.   Auugh! Auugh![25]

---

[25] *Editor's translation:* Nay, nay, thou noble man, thou canst not die,
I'll not allow it, never shall it be.
Thou art too proud for death's dark, humbling fall,
Thou art too good for murder's evil road,
Thou art too witty for death's dismal pall,
Thou art too sly for murder's clumsy step.
This cord of fate I shall untie, reverse,
Pull out the stitches, thread thy life anew,
Rewrite the scene that hath been author'd here
And put thee once more in a starring role.
O, misery beyond a Wookiee's sense—
I had no heart until thou wert my friend,
No mind until I learn'd to think with thee,
No soul until we piloted as one.
How many hours and days have we two shar'd?
How many meals spent laughing in the air?
How many enemies sidestepp'd or dodg'd?
How many loads of treasure smuggl'd we?
O, I shall never know thy like again,
With grief Chewbacca's life shall e'er be fill'd.
If I do smile again, 'twill be too soon,
If I forget thee, galaxies would fall,
If I recover, call me not a friend,
For naught can mend the heart that now doth break.
He was the second half that made me whole,
So I shall go unto my final rest
Imperfect, aye, and incomplete, without
The company of Han—my dearest friend.
I shall with mournful tread now walk the deck.
My captain lies, a'fallen cold and dead.

FINN   —Fine Solo!
REY   —Nay, let this not be;
              O, Han, thou'rt like a father unto me!
                        [Chewbacca, Rey, and Finn begin firing at
                              Kylo Ren and the stormtroopers,
                        who begin shooting back. Chewbacca shoots
                              Kylo Ren in the side, and he stumbles.

KYLO   Foul Wookiee, thou hast hit me in the side,
              Yet I'll be sworn I soon shall have thy hide!   185
                        [Exit Chewbacca. Exeunt Finn
                        and Rey severally. Exeunt Kylo Ren
                              and stormtroopers.

              Enter GENERAL LEIA ORGANA *on balcony,*
              taken aback as she senses that HAN *has died.*

LEIA   [*sings:*] The Force doth move me, works me woe,
              My Han hath fallen, this I know.
              O, death, thou cometh for my Han—
              Sing lackaday, my love is gone.
              Sing hey and lackaday,   190
              My love hath gone away.
              Such torment works within my soul,
              An 'twere I had been shatter'd whole,
              O, Fate, thou cometh for my Han—
              Sing lackaday, my love is gone.   195
              Sing hey and lackaday,
              My love hath gone away.
              My dear, we had too little time,
              To revel in our joy sublime,
              O, end, thou cometh for my Han—   200

Sing lackaday, my love is gone.
Sing hey and lackaday,
My love hath gone away.

[Exit Leia.

SCENE 2.
At Starkiller Base.

Enter REY *and* FINN, *in the snow outside the base.*

FINN
No time have we for ordinary grief,
No time to mourn the loss of our dear Han.
We must unto the *Falcon* make return;
The vile First Order's weapon shall be set
Within two minutes, if I am correct.   5

Enter KYLO REN.

KYLO
Our fight is not complete—ye are for me.
I've just begun to sate my thirst for blood.

REY
Thou art a monster, foul and wretched beast!
Ne'er wert thou worthy to be call'd his son.

KYLO
'Tis but we three. Han Solo cannot help ye.   10
How shalt thou fare without his presence, eh?

REY
Though we are young, still thou shalt know our
                                        might!
Feel thou my fire—

*[Rey tries to shoot Kylo Ren with her
blaster, but he uses the Force to deflect
the shot and pushes her back into a tree.*

She collapses.

KYLO   —Too simple, by my troth.

FINN   O, Rey! Sweet friend, nay. Nay!

KYLO   —Lay on, thou traitor!

[Finn turns on Luke Skywalker's lightsaber.

Yet what is that thou holdest in thy hand?   15
Unwitting as thou art, hast any clue?
That lightsaber wherewith thou plann'st to fight:
It doth belong to me and shall be mine.
Unworthy art thou to unleash its pow'r.

FINN   An thou wouldst take it from me, here I stand.   20

KYLO   Thou hast no skill to use a lightsaber,
Particularly when thou art unfit
To wield the pow'rful weapon in thy hands.
Have at me, then, thou man of ignorance:
I'll give to thee thy first and final lesson.   25

Enter CHORUS.

CHORUS   The two men dodge and parry by their light,
One inexperienc'd, the other train'd.
With savagery and brawn unfolds the fight,
Till Finn by Kylo Ren is sorely pain'd.
He falls and the lightsaber flies aside,   30
Rey wakes nearby—clear thoughts her pain doth
                    smother.
Shall Luke's lightsaber Ren withal abide,
Or shall the Force awaken for another?

[Exit Chorus.
Kylo Ren reaches for the lightsaber,
preparing to use the Force to draw it to him.

KYLO   Now come, lightsaber, to the hand of Ren.
              Fulfill in me thy perfect destiny: 35
              To be constructed by Darth Vader, then
              To fall into the young Skywalker's hands,
              And, at the last, be reunited to
              The dark by this next generation, yea,
              E'en I, call'd Kylo Ren, the grandson and   40
              The heir unto Darth Vader's legacy.
              I feel thy pow'r: now come, for thou art bid.
                              [*The lightsaber flies toward Kylo Ren*
                                      but continues past him,
                                      landing in Rey's hands.

REY   O, hope fulfill'd! O, unexpected Force!
              Come, Kylo Ren, and feel the light of Rey.
                              [*Rey and Kylo Ren freeze*
                                      as they prepare to fight.

              Enter GENERAL HUX *and a* TECHNICIAN
                      above, on balcony.

TECH   But thirty seconds till the weapon hath   45
              Reach'd full capacity, and is prepar'd.
HUX   Prepare to fire and end this vexing fight.
                              [*Exeunt General Hux*
                                      and technician.

              Enter POE DAMERON, YOLO ZIFF, JESS PAVA,
                      and ELLO ASTY *in their ships.*

YOLO   Black Leader, prithee, look! The oscillator
              Doth sport a newfound hole and burneth strong.

	Belike our comrades did their target reach, 50

          Belike our comrades did their target reach,   50

          Delivering the opening we seek.

POE   Let us descend—and strike with all our might.

          This rank Starkiller Base shall fall today!

          Within the oscillator we must fly,

          Move swiftly to pursue our greatest hope: 55

          The weapon wherewith they would strike us down

          Shall fall upon the force of our sharp blasts.

          Aim true, and our defense is made complete—

          Ne'er for a nobler cause have we e'er flown:

          In future times, they shall recall our deeds: 60

          "It was many and many year ago . . ."

          So shall they say, remembering our honor.

          Thus come, my friends, and hallow'd make this day.

          Pray, heed these words of Poe!

PILOTS   —We follow! Aye!

          [Exeunt Poe, Yolo, Jess, and Ello.
             The ground shakes as the base
             begins to self-destruct. Rey and
             Kylo Ren unfreeze as she attacks
             him with vigor. They duel.

KYLO   *[aside:]* She hath more strength that I would ever

                                guess. 65

          Not as one train'd, but like an animal

          She comes at me with brutish energy.

          Still, she hath not the learning to succeed:

          Her inexperience shall be her doom.

REY   *[aside:]* O Finn, O Han, I shall avenge ye both!   70

          This villain shall make answer for his wrongs.

KYLO   *[aside:]* The ground—it shakes an 'twere all nature

                                 did

       Join in our battle, groan with our exertion.
       Ha! Now I press my natural advantage:
       She weakens—she should not have stood to fight. 75
       None so untested and naïve as she
       Shall ever overpower Kylo Ren.
REY   [*aside:*] The ground, it falls away from me. Alack!
       The triumph of the brave Resistance doth
       Mean danger and great risk for those below. 80

        [Kylo Ren forces Rey to the edge of a precipice
         as the ground falls away behind her.

KYLO   I have thee now—thine end shall come anon,
       Unless thou heed'st these gracious words of mine:
       Though thou art strong, I can destroy thee here,
       Yet do I recognize thine aptitude.
       I sense thou need'st a skillful teacher, yea: 85
       Let me show thee the power of the Force!
REY   [*aside:*] O, Force, almost I had forgotten thee.
       Rey, let not vengeance and thine anger fierce
       Keep thee from thinking on what gives thee pow'r.
       Instinct alone this fight can never win, 90
       Not by mine own ability shall I
       O'ercome this man, this brute, this darkest knave.
       Forsooth, 'tis with the Force that I shall live—
       Once it hath call'd in Maz Kanata's castle,
       The steadfast Force hath never left my side. 95
       Hence I did flee, its call I would not heed:
       E'en was I most afeard of what it show'd,
       Repulsive was the vision unto me,
       Jarr'd sharply was my soul by what I saw,
       Elusive visions of the darkness rising. 100
       Distress'd by these unask'd-for mysteries,

I ran away, was ta'en by Kylo Ren.
Now I've the chance to make another choice:
O, Force, I swear I'll run no more from thee,
Where thou shalt lead, from now I'll happ'ly follow.   105
Fear still exists, yet only strengthens me:
Aye, courage is not made by lack of fear.
Respond unto the calling of the Force—
Go, Rey, and give this hateful little man
Occasion to respect the light, the good.   110
No longer scavenger, for I have found
Exactly that which e'er I did desire!
          [Rey counterattacks and drives Kylo Ren
                                  backward.

KYLO   [*aside:*] What is this newfound potency she shows?
           Whence comes this burst of vigor and resolve?

REY   [*aside:*] The Force is with me, sharpen'd in my mind,   115
           It floweth through me an 'twere mine own blood.
           Each move becomes transparent, almost simple,
           As if I knew where Ren would parry next.

KYLO   [*aside:*] Alas, how mortifying in th'extreme!
           My energy grows slack, I must retreat.   120
           The end is clear, but not as I would write it:
           I shall be bested by a scavenger.
                            [Rey strikes Kylo Ren
                         across his face, scarring him.
                            He falls to his knees.

REY   [*aside:*] The Force had led me to this victory,
           Which ends in justice for the innocent.
           For by the end of this most wretched base,   125
           And by the end of this most wretched man,
           Methinks the galaxy shall be secure.

E'en there, I must be careful, by my troth,
For to the dark side I would not be join'd.
If I attempt to slay this humbl'd man,   130
I let the dark side deep inside my heart.
Let me display the mercy he ne'er would.

> [*The ground splits between*
> *Rey and Kylo Ren, forcing*
> *them apart. Exit Kylo Ren.*

Conclusion of this battle is delay'd—
This Kylo Ren and I must meet again.
Now let me fly or share the selfsame fate   135
As this bleak planet, seeming to collapse.

Enter CHEWBACCA *in the* Millennium Falcon.

A-ha, the bold Chewbacca hath return'd
To find both Finn and me and bear us hence.
O, Finn—poor, fallen friend, we'll rescue thee,
And bring to thee what medicines we can   140
In hopes thou, peradventure, shalt recover.
Whatever future Fate for us may braid,
The Force is with me; I'll not be afraid.

Enter POE DAMERON *and other* RESISTANCE PILOTS
in their ships, escorting the Millennium Falcon *away*
from Starkiller Base.

POE   Yea, presently my soul grows stronger for
             They are within my sight! Our task is done,   145
             The battle and the mission all complete.
             Well done, ye company of pilots true—

Let us return anon unto D'Qar!
> *[Exeunt Rey and Chewbacca in the*
> *Millennium Falcon, carrying Finn.*
> *Exeunt Poe and pilots.*

Enter COLONEL DATOO *and a* TECHNICIAN,
who is running away.

DATOO   Say, wherefore dost thou flee without command,
          Lieutenant? Back unto thy station, now!   150
TECH   Nay, we shall not survive, we are undone!
          Canst thou not see the end that comes anon?
          Behold, e'en Gen'ral Hux hath turn'd and fled.
> *[Exeunt Colonel Datoo*
> *and technician, in confusion.*

Enter GENERAL HUX *and* SUPREME LEADER SNOKE
above, on balcony.

HUX   O, Supreme Leader, pray, what shall we do?
          The fuel cells have been ruptur'd past repair,   155
          The planet shall disintegrate anon.
          How it hath happen'd is beyond my mind,
          But by the weak Resistance we are stopp'd.
SNOKE   The fight is o'er for now, the battle lost,
          Yet we shall rise again from this defeat—   160
          The vile Resistance yet shall bear the cost.
          This tempest briefly hath our vessel toss'd,
          The temp'rate waters give off too much heat—
          The fight is o'er for now, the battle lost.
          Pray, leave the base, escape the snow and frost,   165

We shall, anon, plan our revenge complete—
The vile Resistance yet shall bear the cost.
My servant Kylo Ren is double-cross'd:
I sense he hath been, in this instance, beat—
The fight is o'er for now, the battle lost.   170
Though bitter foes our finest do accost,
When Ren is fully train'd, again we'll meet:
The vile Resistance yet shall bear the cost.
Soon the First Order's name shall be emboss'd
On ev'ry soul within th'Resistance fleet.   175
The fight is o'er for now, the battle lost;
The vile Resistance yet shall bear the cost!

[Exeunt General Hux
and Supreme Leader Snoke.

SCENE 3.

At the Resistance base on D'Qar.

Enter CHEWBACCA, *carrying* FINN. *Enter* GENERAL
LEIA ORGANA, REY, C-3PO, BB-8, POE DAMERON, *a* MEDIC,
and several RESISTANCE SOLDIERS. *Enter* R2-D2, *aside.*

MEDIC   He is alive, his heart maintains a beat.
               We shall away, to save him if we can.
                              [Exit medic, bearing away Finn.
                              Leia and Rey walk aside together.
LEIA   Thou hast, in thy young life, seen too much pain.
REY   Thou hast, in thy long life, seen too much pain.
LEIA   Han thought thee brave and strong, a pilot skill'd.   5
REY   Han thought thee strong and brave, a lover true.

LEIA	We both know sorrow and shall mourn for him.
REY	He doth know peace and shall be with us still.
	I bid thee, General, give me thy hand.
LEIA	With it my heart, though rhymeless falls the world. 10
CHEWBAC.	Egh, auugh.[26]
R2-D2	[*aside, awakening:*] —I wake, but what the time and

place?

Ay me, for pity! What a dream was here!
Where is my master Luke? Nearby I see
C-3PO, another droid withal,
A BB unit if my sense is right.   15
I have so long been lock'd in slumber deep
That still I do not trust what I survey.
There is the general, e'en Leia, with
Another woman whom I do not know.
Chewbacca stands thereby, but where is Han?   20
The one is almost never sans the other.
This company is passing strange, indeed:
Full many characters whom I know well,
With other faces I have never seen,
And yet more missing whom I would expect.   25
Dull R2 is unable to make sense,
For after all, I merely am the fool.
Mayhap the fool, though, shall be follow'd yet,
For I have information they may seek.
I'll make my presence known unto them all,   30
Belike to hear their tale and bring new hope.

---

[26] *Editor's translation:* We all are steep'd in misery and joy:
On one hand grieving for our fallen mates,
And on the other marking victory.

          [*To all:*] Meep, beep, beep, squeak, whee, whistle,
                                               whistle, nee!

BB-8   Zooz zzwablay roohblox zzwa, flewflit blavrooh
          Blis bloorooq bluublip zzwazoon flirzoom flit
          Roil zzwablic flew reej zzwa flliblik flig blee!   35

C-3PO   O, R2-D2, thou art all restor'd!
          Thou comest back unto thy friends at last.

R2-D2   Beep, meep, beep, whistle, hoo.

C-3PO   —Thou foundest what?

R2-D2   Meep, beep, beep, squeak!

C-3PO   —O droid intemperate—
          Shalt thou already slander me with words?   40
          How darest thou to call me such a name?

R2-D2	Meep, whistle, hoo, squeak, beep!
C-3PO	—Find Master Luke?

C-3PO   —Find Master Luke?
May it still be? If thou hast information,
I bid thee come and share it with us all.
[To Leia:] O, General, excuse me, General?   45
R2 may have some long-awaited news.

LEIA   R2, to see thee gives my spirit hope.
I bid thee, tell me what thou canst, sweet droid.

R2-D2   *[aside:]* I shall not tell, but show, for as 'tis said,
A picture hath more worth than words—indeed,   50
A thousand words can thereby spoken be.
                [R2-D2 projects a portion of a map.

BB-8   Zood flit zilfrooh blox bleeblay zoomblis zzwablay blip!
                [Poe rushes obtain to the data
                storage unit and gives it to BB-8,
                who projects a map that
                surrounds R2-D2's projection.

C-3PO   The map, it is complete! O, blessèd day.

LEIA   O, Luke, this map—a hologram at most,
A series of faint lines and dots and points—   55
Yet 'tis to me a work of art profound,
For it shall lead us, at the last, to thee.

C-3PO   My lonely days perchance shall be less bleak—
My dearest friend, how I have miss'd thee.

R2-D2   —Squeak!
                     [Exeunt.

SCENE 4.

At the Resistance base on D'Qar.

Enter REY *near* FINN,
who lies unconscious on a pod.
She kisses him on the forehead.

REY   Methinks I shall yearn for thee when I go,
                Yea, thou art such a kind and worthy friend.
                Soon we shall see each other once again:
                This I believe, and thou must too, good Finn.
                O, hear me e'en within thy slumber deep: 5
                Rey owes her life to thee, thou hast her thanks.
                Yet even as I leave thee, prithee know
                I shall return, e'en as thou didst to me.
                Seek we Luke Skywalker, the Jedi true,
                By R2-D2's map, with BB-8's,   10
                Yon shall we fly, and hope to find him there.
                My fondest hopes, my wildest dreams could not
                Yield what I have been call'd herein to do—
                Since I was but a lowly scavenger,
                There on the dismal planet of Jakku,   15
                Expected I that I would live and die
                Restricted by my past, my constant wait:
                Yearn would I for those who would never come.
                Considering where I began, my roots,
                Out of all expectation I have flown.   20
                My fate hath spun beyond what I'd believe:
                Plac'd deep within the brave Resistance's ranks,
                Initiated in the pow'rful Force.

Lo, with Chewbacca and R2 I go,
E'en in the swift *Millenn'um Falcon* fly,   25
Determining the future of my life.

Enter GENERAL LEIA ORGANA. *Enter* CHEWBACCA,
R2-D2, C-3PO, BB-8, POE DAMERON,
and RESISTANCE SOLDIERS *aside,*
preparing the Millennium Falcon *for departure.*

LEIA   Rey, may the Force be with thee as thou goest.
               [They embrace.

C-3PO   For now the tale hath come unto its end,
A mixture of emotions bittersweet.
The Force begins to waken in th'Resistance,   30
A new hope is reveal'd to us at last.

REY   New friends were made by these adventures here,
New chances for a better life obtain'd,
New consciousness unto the mighty Force,
New ways to serve our hurting galaxy.   35

LEIA   Along the way, we lost a noble man:
My love, a scoundrel and a warrior.
Our star wars face a newfound enemy,
What cometh next is mystery to me.

Enter CHORUS *as epilogue.*

CHORUS   Young Rey, Chewbacca, and the droid R2   40
Pursue the map the droids did make complete.
Through space they fly with lightspeed's blazing hue
In hopes that they Luke Skywalker shall meet.
Unto an unknown system do they fly,

Wherein an island sits in ocean deep.   45
They land the ship, debark, and, by and by,
Rey mounts the steps toward a mountain steep.
Thereon she finds a man in robe of gray,
Who turns to her his bearded, wizen'd face:
It is the Jedi, Luke Skywalker, yea—   50
Rey offers him his lightsaber with grace.
There end we—the next chapter we await:
'Twill come as sure as seven leads to eight.

[Exeunt omnes.

END.

AFTERWORD.

Like everyone else, I awaited December 17, 2015, with excitement and anticipation. Unlike everyone else, as I watched the movie I was thinking, "Hmm, there could be a soliloquy there . . ." "How will I stage that scene?" "I could have fun with that character . . ." (For the record, I saw *The Force Awakens* four times in the theater. Some of you will laugh at that because it's so many, and others scoff because it's so few.)

William Shakespeare's The Force Doth Awaken was great fun to write because I was able to revisit favorite characters from the original trilogy and introduce new characters to the Shakespeare's *Star Wars* series. Of course, a new cast of characters means new opportunities to play with language. I won't give everything away, but here are some hints to what I did: Rey's longer soliloquies reference the many fan theories of her heritage; every line Finn speaks includes the letters of his stormtrooper name; each of Poe's lines includes a phrase from the verses of a famous Poe-t; and all of BB-8's lines can be deciphered if you know the (skip) code.

Among the new characters are new villains. A while back, Erik Didriksen (author of *Pop Sonnets*) and I tossed around the idea of a collection of "Villain Villanelles," that is, a group of poems written about or from the perspective of various well-known villains from literature and film, each conforming to the structure and rhyme scheme of a villanelle. We didn't get very far with the project, but I resurrected the idea in *William Shakespeare's The Force Doth Awaken*. Each of the three main villains in this book—Kylo Ren, General Hux, and Supreme Leader Snoke—speaks one villanelle during the story.

The characters from the original trilogy who return in *William*

Shakespeare's The Force Doth Awaken keep their conventions from the previous books: Han and Leia speak in rhyming quatrains; Admiral Ackbar's lines end in an *-ap* sound; and R2-D2 speaks in English in asides to the audience. One change from my earlier books is that I finally give Chewbacca his due. That's something I've wanted to do for a while, and it's especially appropriate given the loss he suffers in this episode.

Speaking of loss, while this book was being finished, the wonderful, charismatic, and outrageous Carrie Fisher died. It was a sad day for *Star Wars* fans everywhere, and we will all miss our beloved Leia, who, as Lor San Tekka states, is royalty. As Shakespeare said, "Now cracks a noble heart. Good night, sweet princess: and flights of angels sing thee to thy rest!"

Onward and upward to Episode VIII! People often ask me if I see the *Star Wars* scripts early or get advance knowledge of the plot. Nope. I experience the movies just like you, as a fan sitting in a movie theater wondering what will happen next. Look for me—I'll be the one with his head bent at a funny angle, mumbling, "How would Shakespeare do this?"

ACKNOWLEDGMENTS.

This book is dedicated to my nieces, Aracelli, Addison, and Sophie. They bring a smile to my face whenever I see them. Their parents—Erik and Em, Joel and Sibyl—are doing good work.

To my family, as always, a deep thank-you for supporting me: my parents, Bob and Beth; my brother Erik and his family; and my aunt Holly. Thank you to my friend Josh Hicks, the person I text, email, and call when I need to geek out. Thank you to his wife, Alexis Kaushansky, and baby Ruby, who don't mind. Thank you, Murray Biggs, my former professor and current friend, for adding greatly to my knowledge of Shakespeare's language (though he'll be quick to point out that all the mistakes are mine). Thank you to the amazing team at Quirk Books: Jason Rekulak, Rick Chillot, Nicole De Jackmo, Brett Cohen, Christina Schillaci, Jane Morley, Tim O'Donnell, Doogie Horner, and the rest of the crew. Thank you to Nicolas Delort for delightful illustrations.

Thank you to all the others who have touched these projects and supported me as I wrote: Heidi Altman and Scott Roehm, Heather Antos, Jack and Judy Bevilacqua, Jane Bidwell, Travis Boeh and Sarah Woodburn, Chris Buehler and Marian Hammond, Erin and Nathan Buehler, Melody and Jason Burton, Jeff and Caryl Creswell, Kathy Douglass, Jeanette Ehmke, Mark Fordice, Tom George and Kristin Gordon, Jim and Nancy Hicks, Anne Huebsch, Apricot, David, Isaiah and Oak Irving, Jerryn Johnston, Bobby Lopez, Chris and Andrea Martin, Bruce McDonald, Joan and Grady Miller, Jim Moiso, Michael Morrill and Tara Schuster, Lucy and Tim Neary, Dave Nieuwstraten, Omid Nooshin, Bill Rauch, Julia Rodriguez-O'Donnell, Helga and Michael Scott, Naomi Walcott and Audu Besmer, Ryan, Nicole, Mackinzie, Audrey and Lily Warne-McGraw,

Steve Weeks, Jordan White, Ryan Wilmot, Ben and Katie Wire, Ethan Youngerman and Rebecca Lessem, and Dan Zehr.

My spouse, Jennifer, is a constant source of inspiration and love—thank you, Jennifer. Thank you to my son Liam, who learned to play the *Star Wars* theme song on the piano just for me. Finally, a HUGE thank-you to my son Graham, who let me borrow his *Star Wars: The Force Awakens Visual Dictionary*, without which I could not have written this book!

William Shakespeare's
Star Wars: Verily, A New Hope

COLLECT THE

William Shakespeare's
The Empire Striketh Back

William Shakespeare's
The Jedi Doth Return

William Shakespeare's
The Phantom of Menace

E N T I R E   S A G A !

William Shakespeare's
The Clone Army Attacketh

William Shakespeare's
Tragedy of the Sith's Revenge

SONNET 2187
"The First Order of Business . . ."

No resolution hath the seventh part
Of our beloved *Star Wars* history.
Young Rey hath both a heavy fate and heart
Her character enwrapp'd in mystery.
Bold Finn, the former trooper, doth endure,
Though by an injury his story's clouded.
And Kylo Ren—with motives still impure—
In hate and darkness is completely shrouded.
Yet though the book is done, more shall betide;
On Quirk Books' website, find thou something fresher:
There thou shalt see an **educators' guide**
And **interview** with author Ian Doescher.
Online—**quirkbooks.com**—yea, so said I!
We'll meet again beyond *The Last Jedi.*

quirkbooks.com/theforcedothawaken